0 6 SEP 2021

Falkirk
Community
Trust

KU-750-405

HIS DAUGHTER'S DUTY

Lucinda is in an arranged marriage with a man she doesn't understand. They share a dispassionate camaraderie, but gradually her opinion begins to change. When his life is endangered her feelings intensify — ones that she's trying to ignore . . . Laurence's father taunted him with the words 'second choice'. Love is irrelevant until Lucinda captures his heart. He decides to beg her for a second chance and hopes she realizes his motives are not from a sense of obligation.

WENDY KREMER

HIS DAUGHTER'S DUTY

Complete and Unabridged

LINFORD
Leicester

First published in Great Britain in 2019

First Linford Edition
published 2020

A catalogue record for this book is available
from the British Library.

ISBN 978–1–4448–4578–5

Published by
Ulverscroft Limited
Anstey, Leicestershire

Set by Words & Graphics Ltd.
Anstey, Leicestershire
Printed and bound in Great Britain by
T. J. International Ltd., Padstow, Cornwall

This book is printed on acid-free paper

Shock Proposal

She hadn't received many callers since her father's death, and certainly didn't reckon on Laurence Ellesporte calling to express his sympathy. John brought her his card, and stated that the gentleman would like to see her, if it was convenient. She rose quickly, straightened her dress, and followed him downstairs.

She found her visitor's lean form folded into one of the stiff chairs next to the unlit fireplace. Lord Laurence Ellesporte rose and bowed when she entered. He sat down again as soon as she was sitting opposite. Lucinda tightened her hands in her lap and looked down for a second to steady her thoughts.

Her father and this man's father had not been on speaking terms for many years. The old Lord Ellesporte had died two years before.

The two men had always acted as if

the other estate and its owner didn't exist. Lucinda looked up, met Ellesporte's direct gaze and straightened her shoulders.

Laurence was a formidable figure. She estimated he was mid-thirties with broad shoulders, an athletic figure, ascetic features and dark piercing eyes.

He wore a closely tailored dark jacket, a high-collared white shirt, and a perfectly knotted white cravat.

Lucinda had never had a London season, but even she could tell his attire was of the finest quality and made with masterly skill.

'May I offer you some refreshments, my lord?'

His expression relaxed slightly.

'No, thank you. I came to express my sympathy.'

She nodded. It still hurt. She pulled herself together.

He deliberated before he spoke again.

'I hope you'll not consider me lacking in the social niceties if I ask when it will be convenient to talk about the agreement?'

2

'Agreement? What agreement?' she asked, puzzled. 'I'm sorry, sir, but I don't know what you're talking about.'

His brow furrowed as he viewed her puzzled expression. An appalling thought crossed his brain as he considered her guileless expression.

'You know nothing of our parents' arrangement?'

Lucinda shook her head.

'No. Your father and mine were long-standing, bitter adversaries. My father never mentioned your father's name, or any arrangement. He would have, if it were important.

'Has it to do with sharing the lower fields for grazing? That was always a bone of contention. What is this agreement about?' Lucinda prayed it had nothing to do with money. It was already impossible to make ends meet.

Laurence shifted, and brushed invisible fluff from his black knee-breeches. He felt uncomfortable and he silently cursed her father for not explaining things before he died. A muscle in his cheek twitched. His austere features displayed little kindness when he replied.

'It's extremely unfortunate that your father didn't inform you about this agreement.' He paused for a second before continuing. 'Miss Harting . . . our fathers planned that we should marry and unite the two estates.'

Lucinda was already very pale from the effort of nursing her father. Now any remaining colour disappeared completely. The shock of his words made her feel faint. She steadied and held her head high.

'You're mistaken, my lord,' she replied, her voice shaking. 'I'm sure my father would never want me to marry into your family.

'I'm in the happy position of not having to marry. This estate is not entailed, and I am the sole inheritor.'

Laurence viewed her ghostlike appearance. He was not hostile towards her, he merely felt extremely annoyed.

'You haven't yet spoken to your family solicitor? He should have explained everything, after your father's funeral.'

4

'No, we haven't spoken. He was taken ill, and was unable to attend the funeral. He's due the day after tomorrow.'

Why should he soften the facts if her own father hadn't made the effort?

'Your lawyer will inform you that this estate has debt, enormous debt, accumulated over many years. My father picked up those debts.

'When your father saw there was no hope of repayment, he agreed to my father's suggestion. Either the debts were settled immediately on your father's death, or we marry and amalgamate the two estates.' Laurence extracted a Sevres snuffbox and took a pinch.

'I don't wish to be indelicate, Miss Harting, but I don't think you're able to settle those debts, are you?'

Lucinda was determined not to get hysterical.

'I don't believe you, sir. I don't have to marry. I repeat, the estate is not entailed, it's mine. If what you say is true, I'll sell part of Greystone to clear the debts.

'This is my home. I'll not give it away because of a mad agreement between your father and mine. My father's debts will be repaid in full, sir.' She stood up, her eyes blazing.

Laurence was silently impressed that she hadn't fainted and keeled over. Her sense of fashion was appalling but she had bravado, delicate features and a pretty face.

He sighed.

'Madam, please listen. The estate may be yours, but in name only. The debts now almost exceed its worth. My father deposited all those obligations with his lawyer along with his instructions. Your father was not a gambler but he was a bad manager, and he invested in the wrong things. He did repay small amounts now and then, but it never scratched the surface.'

He seemed indifferent to how the news might affect her. His expression was not malicious, merely aloof.

'You can, of course, declare yourself bankrupt,' he continued. 'The present law means I could then have you imprisoned for outstanding debts.'

Lucinda flinched and he hastily reassured her.

'I would not go to such extremes, and I know nothing of your personal circumstances, but unless you have a sympathetic relation who is prepared to maintain you for the rest of your life, you'll find yourself dispossessed and as poor as a church mouse.'

'But . . . ' She struggled to respond. 'But surely you don't agree to this farce? I promise to repay the debts — even if it takes a lifetime. The whole idea is stupid. We've never met before. You know nothing about me or my uneventful life, and I've only heard gossip about the kind of life you lead, in London.'

Laurence interrupted her remark.

'Most of which is untrue and fabricated. Anyway, what difference does that make?'

'Surely you don't wish to marry me, sir?' she retorted impatiently. 'We come from different circles, and are governed by different circumstances.' She eyed him openly. 'My lord, I would bore you to tears in five minutes!'

'Arranged marriages to increase the size of one's property are not unusual, even in this day and age,' he drawled. He decided to show more compassion, as he considered her bewildered expression.

'My dear child, I'm just as displeased about this abominable arrangement, but my hands are tied. Stop considering your own position, and consider mine. My father told me of this agreement before he died. I had to swear to abide by, and uphold, the agreement. If I didn't, I'd be disinherited.

'He must have hated your father very much,' he continued. 'He was probably jealous of his standing locally. We're not merely talking about your position, we're also talking about me losing an immense fortune. I'm afraid I'm too level-headed to throw away my inheritance by refusing to marry you.

'If you refuse to marry me, I still get

your estate, because of the extent of the debt, but I'll have kept my side of the bargain . . . I'd then be free to do as I wish — marry anyone I like. I may add, at present, I wasn't planning to marry anyone.

'Even if Greystone was debt-free, how could you run it on your own?

'I don't think you have much choice, have you? If you refuse, I'll retain my possessions, and you'll be an unattached female pauper. It's no hardship for me to comply with my father's wishes, because my life will continue exactly as before. I'd be a fool to reject it.

'If you refuse, you'll probably end up as someone's poor companion, or as a downtrodden governess. I might occasionally think how my family was the cause of your downfall and poverty, but not very often, I can assure you.'

'You'd marry me just to hang on to money?' Lucinda gasped. He remained silent and met her glance. 'There must be a solution. Why did your father hate mine so much?'

He shrugged.

'I have no idea. I never asked. My father hated many people. In fact, I think he disliked me most of the time, too. He was a peculiar man.' He trifled with the pince-nez hanging on a ribbon round his neck.

Her eyes were drawn to his well-groomed long hands with their buffed fingernails.

Lucinda tried to think calmly.

'If Greystone has large debts and is badly managed, surely it will only be a financial liability for you, for some time.'

He eyed her carefully through half-closed lids.

'Contrary to what people believe, I do follow the affairs of my estates and properties very carefully. I check new developments in agriculture and make sure my agents are progressive thinkers and any stewardship is carried out intelligently.

'I didn't collect those debts by using my own money. It was done by my father with his, therefore the debts will be no loss to me if they remain unpaid. I can rip them up and simply tell my manager to go ahead.

'He'll turn things around quite easily within a couple of years. The estate was badly managed, but its potentials are excellent. Your father never had any spare money to employ someone who knew what he was doing.'

Lucinda knew that was true. During the last couple of years, her father's interest was practically non-existent. People who rented some of their holdings never accepted her spoken suggestions.

In the end, she'd resorted to letters and messages. Although her father signed those directives, they generally fell on deaf ears. She realised an estate that wanted to employ innovative agricultural ideas needed personal supervision and cajolery.

'You can't possibly want to marry me, sir — not even to gain another estate.'

His brows raised and he continued to play moodily with his silver quizzing glass. He shrugged.

'Why not? The owners of large estates often intermarry to increase their fortunes. I'll have to marry one day, and it's all the same to me who she is. As long as you don't cramp my style in London, I'll be perfectly happy to leave you here in the country.'

She tried to hide her dismay and shock.

'You don't care who she is, as long as she doesn't interfere in your lifestyle? You'll be happy if you lead separate lives?'

His expression was inscrutable.

'What's wrong with that? The majority of marriages end up like that anyway. When I observe married couples I know, I often wonder why they married in the first place. They sit next to each other like marble statues with nothing to say, and nothing in common.'

'But you need an heir,' she retorted, blushing furiously.

He waved his long fingers in a gesture of dismissal.

'That's true, I suppose. It's a point we'll have to agree on, but there's no rush.' Lucinda bristled but remained silent.

'Let's not dwell on such things at present. I suggest that you listen to what your father's lawyer says, and then decide what you want to do.

'Perhaps there is a cosy haven you can escape to within your family circle — that's if you decide marrying me is too disastrous a notion.'

'It's not only disastrous, it's insulting,' she retorted with heightened colour. 'We look after and sell our cows with more care than how this arrangement was managed.'

Laurence stifled his laughter.

'You're right. You're very right!' His eyes twinkled for a brief moment then he rose. 'I would not have come this morning if I knew you had no inkling of what our parents had arranged. I didn't choose to be the bringer of this information, madam, but at least you are now forewarned of what your father's lawyer will relate.' He looked around. 'It seems your father's lawyer, like so many other things on this estate, needs shaking up.'

Her lips drew into a straight line.

'Mr Willoughby was ill, sir. He didn't intentionally drag his feet. He has always been kind and concerned. He was my father's lifelong lawyer.'

He bowed curtly.

'Then perhaps this kind and concerned man should have warned your father more judiciously about how the agreement would vex you. He has, in fact, been a contributing factor in leaving you in an uncomfortable and confusing position.

'I wish you good day, and ask you to contact me when you have decided. I'm returning to London this afternoon, but my agent at Castleward will always forward important messages. As you're in mourning, there is no compulsion to marry immediately . . . that's if you agree.' He turned on his heel.

Lucinda followed him out and

viewed the back of his head. His hair was perfectly arranged, and tied with a black ribbon. He accepted his hat and gloves from John with a nod.

Without a backward glance, he strode towards the entrance door. John hurried to open it in time for him to exit.

As Laurence Ellesporte took the reins of his phaeton, he mused that at least she was not one of those clinging females who needed to be led by a stronger will. He had the feeling Miss Harting was self-reliant and that would mean he'd be free to remain independent and unconfined.

Left With No Choice

Lucinda returned to the salon and sat down. Her legs were still unsteady. She hoped she hadn't shown him how frightened she felt. He was an abominable man without feeling! What should she do?

Once she felt calmer, she realised she should not have agreed to see him without a suitable companion. Her old nurse was her closest companion, but Annie had declared long ago that she was too nervous to be in the presence of the aristocracy.

Any visitors who vaguely fell into this category were always received in the presence of her father. Any local friends knew they could call and socialise with her without restrictions. In London, it was probably an dreadful faux-pas for any man to be alone in a room with an unmarried woman. Good! Perhaps that would show him just how unsuitable she was.

John coughed to attract her attention. 'Everything is well, Miss Lucinda? He seems to be a very fine gentleman.'

Lucinda knew it was not proper to discuss private concerns with servants, but John had served her father before she was born, and he was very protective.

'Yes, it was a great surprise.' She would talk to Willoughby before she mentioned the real reason of Ellesporte's visit to anyone, even to Annie.

John's voice remained discreet when he spoke again.

'An Ellesporte calling to show his sympathy? Things are indeed improving, miss. There was no contact in your father's time.'

Lucinda didn't reply.

'Will you ask Annie for some chocolate in ten minutes, please? I'm just going upstairs to get a book.'

She considered her figure in the large gilt mirror as she crossed the square hallway. Black didn't suit her. She and Annie had altered her mother's old mourning wear.

It was completely out-of-date, of course, and even after they'd undone all the seams and then restyled the black silk into a straight high-waisted dress with short French sleeves, and a couple of decorative black flounces on the hem, the result was far from flattering.

She straightened her dark grey spencer, touched her braided hair, and hurried up the broad staircase.

Annie was dyeing two of her old day dresses this morning. She'd have to wear mourning for some months yet, and needed more than this one dress for the coming days and weeks ahead.

Fortunately, her father had never encouraged visitors to Greystone. His death was a plausible excuse to refuse any invitations she received to attend any social events in the locality.

There was no spare money for buying new mourning clothes for such occurrences. The corners of her mouth turned up when she considered the impression she must have made on Laurence Ellesporte. Her expression dimmed again as she recalled his words.

As she strode down the upstairs corridor, she wondered what type of woman he preferred. According to Mrs Stevenson and Juliet, blondes were all the rage in London this season.

She entered her father's room, the stiff silk of her dress rustling as she moved. She found comfort for a moment, amongst the things her father used and loved.

There was a portrait of her mother above the mantelpiece. Lucinda couldn't remember her. She died of inflammation of the lungs when Lucinda was two.

She studied the picture. Her mother was tall and slender with dark chestnut hair and brown eyes. Her father always told her she reminded him of her mother and that she was just as pretty, but he was prejudiced.

She recalled Lord Ellesporte's words. The only close relative who could help was Uncle Henry. He was her deceased aunt's husband, a scholar who wrote books about long forgotten civilisations.

As a younger son, he inherited a small annuity from his mother, and he owned a small house in Portsmouth. He'd attended Father's funeral and gone home over ten days ago. Lucinda didn't think he would welcome an addition to his household. He was too introverted and set in his ways. Her aunt had loved him dearly, and they lived in harmony together without the need for much entertaining, travelling or extravagances.

What would become of John, Annie, Willy, Adam the old gardener, Mrs Wilson the cook, Lily, their only maid, and the women from the village who did the cleaning and the washing? Some of those women were widows with small children, and had no other means of support.

Greystone wasn't a large house in comparison to Castleward, but it still required care and attention. John,

Annie, and Adam wouldn't find new work, they were too old, and they might end their days in the poorhouse. She licked her lips and realised that her decision to accept or not would affect them all.

She looked in the dressing-table mirror and pinched her cheeks. She looked deathly pale and her dress hung loosely on her slim shape. She straightened and picked up a novel from her father's writing desk. It was the book she read to him as he lay fighting for his life. She hurried out of the room again.

When she reached the salon, Annie was just placing a cup of steaming chocolate on a side table.

'There you are, sweetheart. Drink it before it gets cold.'

Lucinda smiled at her.

'Thank you, Annie. Mr Willoughby will be staying for the night when he comes tomorrow. His room is ready?'

'All organised and ready. I sent Willy out to catch a rabbit in the corpse down by the river. We have trout from the stream, a chicken pie, a trifle and some macaroons all ready.'

'Good.'

'Drink the chocolate and rest by the fire this afternoon. You're too thin and you look tired.'

Lucinda stroked her hand.

'Thank you. I'm fine.'

'You spent too many days nursing your father, and then there was the formality of his funeral. It's not surprising you look tired.'

'He needed me, Annie. I was glad to be there.'

She fell asleep, and after the evening meal, she went to bed early thinking she would muse about her future. She fell asleep again as soon as her head touched the pillow.

* * *

When Mr Willoughby arrived, she was in the kitchen garden. It was just beginning to produce the vegetables they needed and enjoyed so much. He came to look for her. His smile calmed her and they talked of inconsequential things until he suggested they return to the library to complete the official business.

There, he told her she was owner of the estate but there was no money. That was expected, but then he began to repeat Lord Ellesporte's words. Her throat was dry.

'I can't believe my father agreed to it.'

He nodded.

'I understand, but I'll try to explain. I knew your father all his life. He didn't want to get into debt. The fight went out of him when your mother died and after that, he was careless and easy-going. Money lenders soon saw their chance.'

He saw the dismay in her eyes and touched her hand briefly.

'When Lord Ellesporte's lawyer contacted him with his suggestion, we talked about the situation several times. In the end your father and I both decided it would be to your advantage.'

'To my advantage?' she spluttered.

'Miss Harting, if you marry Lord Ellesporte, you'll be secure for the rest of your life. Your father was extremely worried about the mounting debt and leaving you destitute. When he discovered old Lord Ellesporte was holding all the obligations, he grew more fearful.

'He intended to tell you, but his death was so unexpected. He enquired about the young Lord Ellesporte whenever he visited London to see me, and heard nothing averse. Laurence Ellesporte is respected, no gambler, a first-rate sportsman, and well-connected. We decided such a marriage would be an excellent match, especially as you have no dowry.'

Her eyes were too bright, and her voice was brittle.

'He should have told me, Mr Willoughby.'

'He kept putting it off. He didn't want you to see he wasn't capable of running an estate or caring for his daughter. In the end, he believed he could convince you that it was right for you. He comforted himself with knowing that if you were Lady Ellesporte, it was something you could never hope to achieve under normal circumstances without an immense dowry.'

She rose quickly.

'You were planning my future life, Mr Willoughby.'

He rose and eyed her sympathetically.

'I know it is a shock, but allow me to point out that you now need the security and protection of a home and a husband. A daughter always has to accept her parents' choice of a husband. Your father doted on you, but he would have chosen someone for you one day. He worried about you being alone and vulnerable.

'It's an excellent match. Lord Ellesporte is extremely rich, he'll treat you well, he's comely to look at, and a renowned sportsman. I've heard nothing bad of him. When you reflect on it, I'm sure you'll see the advantage of such a marriage.'

Lucinda pushed back the chair and hurried out of the room. Reaching the garden, she let the tears fall.

She knew she had no choice. Despondently, she mused that she was too sensible to end up being penniless and a burden to her uncle, or being an impoverished governess. She worried about would happen to the servants, too, as they were now her responsibility.

Lucinda deliberated for a few days but found no other solution. She sent Laurence a curt message, and requested him to commence the formalities.

He replied just as curtly stating, unless she objected, he'd arrange to attend her in ten days' time with both of their lawyers.

A Cold Arrangement

Highly nervous and slightly embarrassed, Lucinda waited with Uncle Henry and Mr Willoughby in the library at Greystone.

Her uncle had been shocked when he heard how much his brother-in-law was indebted, and about the subsequent arrangements he'd made with Lord Ellesporte.

'It's very disturbing, Lucinda. I didn't know all this when Lord Ellesporte called briefly last week to ask for my permission. He mentioned nothing about the debts or the agreement.

'As I'm your nearest relative, it was proper of him to call. He assured me you had agreed to your betrothal, and it was your father's wish, I didn't hesitate to give permission . . . Anyway, he's not the kind of man I could refuse easily.

Lord Ellesporte will give you security and an appropriate place in society, but that will mean little unless you respect each other.

'I can only offer you a roof over your head if you refuse, and you're unlikely ever to receive a similar offer again. You know I take no part in social entertainments and that will not change.

'I own little for you to inherit, but if you're set against this marriage . . .'

Lucinda shook her head. She knew there was no real alternative.

'I've accepted his proposal, Uncle Henry,' she replied softly.

As they waited, the two men filled the time talking about politics until the sound of a carriage was heard. They waited for John's announcement.

Obviously, Ellesporte's lawyer knew all the details. His expression was bland but there was benevolence when he shook Lucinda's hand and before he sat down.

Laurence acknowledged her by lifting her hand to his lips briefly without touching the surface. He was as well-dressed as ever and his expression just as non-committal. His cutaway was of dark blue and a waistcoat of silver and grey peeped out from behind a necktie in the waterfall style.

He bowed to the two men and viewed them through narrow lids before sitting down. His dark eyes were watchful.

She concentrated her thoughts, looked down, and noted the poor quality of her dress. She was an unassuming and wholly unsuitable figure for her illustrious future husband.

His lawyer cleared his throat and proceeded to read their marriage agreement. The legal jargon made it sound complicated, but Lucinda understood that she'd receive four hundred pounds pin-money annually. She was shocked by the generous amount but did not show it.

In the event of Laurence's death without an heir, she would re-inherit Greystone Hall and its lands and a distant cousin would inherit Castleward.

Greystone became his property through

their marriage. There was no mention of a dowry but that was not surprising. Greystone Hall had nothing to offer except debts and its mistress.

Lucinda guessed that normally the bride-to-be was not present at such a meeting, but Mr Willoughby told her Lord Ellesporte had suggested she should be there.

The wedding would take place within eight weeks. Uncle Henry signed, Laurence signed, and the business was completed. The two lawyers and Uncle Henry got up to share a glass of wine.

Lucinda and Laurence sat facing each other.

'I hope you're well, Lucinda?' he asked.

'Thank you, my lord. I am very well.'

He smiled.

'Tut! Tut! We are betrothed. You must call me Laurence. It would be very strange if you don't.'

She hesitated and coloured.

'Oh, yes, forgive me. I still find it difficult to adjust.' He nodded with a look of understanding that surprised her.

'I wondered if our marriage will seem unacceptable, as I'm living in Greystone on my own, without a guardian,' she said.

'As you have never had a London season and are only known locally I don't think anyone is likely to think that strange. I am not acquainted with many people hereabout, but they know you well enough to realise no disrespect to your father is intended by either of us.'

'Another thing, Laurence.' His name didn't flow easily — she had to concentrate.

'Yes?' He took a pinch of snuff and cast his eye around the room.

'What about Greystone Hall?'

He seemed puzzled.

'Greystone Hall? What do you mean?'

'If you're going to live in London, do I live here or in Castleward?'

'Oh, Castleward I should imagine,' he answered, sounding a little bored. 'As my wife you should be in charge there.'

'That's what I expected,' she said, biting her lip, 'but what about Greystone Hall?' She paused. 'I wondered if I might invite Uncle Henry to live here. He needs peaceful surroundings for his work, so it would be ideal for him. It would also be nice for me to have him living nearby.'

She didn't mention the real reason because Laurence Ellesporte probably never gave much thought to his servants. If Uncle Henry lived in Greystone there would be a plausible reason to keep the servants.

'Do as you wish. To be honest, apart from leasing it to someone on a permanent basis or as a summer residence, I don't know what we can do with it. Probably my agent will be glad he doesn't have to bother. He'll have enough to do, getting the land and the holdings back into shape.'

Lucinda smothered her relief.

'Good. I'll suggest it to Uncle Henry. It is better than leaving the place empty. I'll move to Castleward.'

His glance wandered round the meagre choice of books.

'Greystone looks like it needs a bit of renovation,' he commented.

'There was never much spare money. Anyway, men don't notice such things. Uncle Henry won't, I'm sure.'

'You're wrong, Lucinda,' he said, viewing her through his quizzing glass. 'This particular man, for one, does. By the way, I hope you don't want the rigmarole of a lavish wedding? I intend to get a special licence and, apart from the clergyman, your Uncle Henry, and a friend of mine, I don't require anyone else to be there. Are you agreed?'

She nodded.

'People from Greystone might turn up at the church out of respect to wish me well, but I prefer a quiet ceremony, too.'

'Good! That's settled then.' He stood up and looked across to his lawyer. 'I'm due back in London for an important meeting tomorrow afternoon.' He looked down at her.

'You can choose the day and time. A special licence allows any time and any place. Just let me know when I should turn up.

'I'll tell my housekeeper at Castleward to expect you. Take a look around before we marry. If you find something is not to your taste, you're welcome to re-decorate. After all, you'll live there, not me.

'Don't worry about the future. I don't. I've found that fate often straightens a bend. Perhaps you'll find that being mistress of Castleward will compensate for the inconvenience of being my wife.'

'Do you entertain friends at Castleward?' she suddenly asked.

He paused, as if to think about it.

'Well, there have been a couple of parties, but very seldom. If it does happen, you'll be free to join your Uncle Henry for a few days if you don't want to stay. I'm sure my friends won't find it strange if you're not sitting at the head of the table.'

Lucinda's mind was in a whirl. He

was an unusual character. She knew nothing about marriages among the nobility but, to her, the idea of living apart seemed a scatter-brained way to conduct a marriage.

His lips turned upward in a barely discernible parting smile before he left.

'Good day, Lucinda.'

She dipped her head in answer and decided it might not be so bad to be married to Laurence Ellesporte after all. It looked like he was leaving her to her own devices, and if visitors came to Castleward, she had a loophole to escape. It would be polite to greet his guests, but then she could come to Greystone Hall and ignore happenings at Castleward until they left.

She'd try to be a good mistress. She'd never been inside Castleward and only seen it from a distance. She hoped she was equal to the task. Perhaps it would be a very good idea to visit before their marriage, and introduce herself to the housekeeper. If the housekeeper was on her side, everything would be a great deal easier. It was never sensible to have your housekeeper as an adversary.

With a Heavy Heart

The intervening weeks had passed too fast. The small church, attached to the main house at Castleward, was cold. Uncle Henry and Laurence's friend were talking in the aisle, and Lucinda was delighted when she saw the Stevensons had come, too. They sat in the shadows at the back. She felt nervous and shivered. Laurence had brought the dergyman with him.

Soon, she found herself repeating her vows.

'I, Lucinda Mary Harting, take thee, Laurence Ross Ellesporte, to my wedded husband.' The words echoed through the ancient stone building. She had determined beforehand not to whisper. That would appear she was frightened — and even if she was, she wasn't going to show it.

Laurence repeated his vows, and

pushed the heavy wedding ring on to her finger.

'With this ring I thee wed, with my body I thee honour, and with all my worldly goods I thee endow.'

He didn't look at her once during the ceremony, and it was over quickly. The Stevensons were gone by the time they'd signed the papers. Lucinda was touched when she exited the church on his arm to find that John and Annie were waiting. They showered them with flower petals and wished them well.

Annie kissed her cheek and bobbed at Laurence.

'Forgive us for interrupting, my lord, but we've known Lucinda all her life, and John and I wanted to wish her happiness.'

Lucinda's eyes misted over. She knew how much courage it must have cost Annie to speak to him. Laurence acknowledged her politely.

John kissed her cheek and they then carried on towards the main building. The servants were all gathered in the hall, and they clapped when the bridal pair walked in.

Lucinda could tell that Laurence had not expected a reception, but he reacted instantaneously and shook hands with his personal valet, Timothy. He nodded to the butler.

'Everyone gets something special to drink this evening, William. Thank you,' he added, addressing them all. 'I hope you'll support my wife in the same way you have supported me.'

As they continued on to the main drawing-room, Laurence's friend Guy whispered in his ear.

'Where's the clergyman?'

'I told him there is a carriage waiting to carry him to the next post station after the wedding. He's probably on his way back to London by now.'

Uncle Henry followed them. He looked with approval at what he saw. It was clear that no money was being spared to make Castleward one of the most impressive houses he had ever seen. Lucinda was fortunate.

They entered the drawing-room where settees and chairs covered in thick green brocade were scattered around the room. The cream marble fireplace was framed on either side by large family portraits.

Lucinda was delighted to find the piano she'd noticed in one of the side rooms had been moved here. She had casually mentioned to the housekeeper, Mrs Wilson, that she loved playing the piano and Mrs Wilson had thus responded. Laurence lowered his arm and she was released. Mrs Wilson had laid a small buffet on a side-table and champagne was cooling on ice. She curtseyed.

'I wish you and your new bride every happiness, your lordship.'

'Thank you for your good wishes, Mrs Wilson — and also for the fare and champagne. I didn't think of it, but you're right. We must celebrate.'

Mrs Wilson withdrew and Laurence picked up the champagne bottle and filled some elegant flutes. Lucinda moved to the windows overlooking the formal gardens at the back of the house. Laurence handed her a glass and, raising his glass to her, he admired her tawny eyes.

'It's appropriate to toast my wife and this special day.'

Guy and Uncle Henry echoed his words with raised glasses.

Lucinda was grateful that Laurence was playing his part to perfection, probably for Uncle Henry's sake. Laurence moved to Uncle Henry's side and they began to talk about the hunting season, and where the best fishing in the locality was. It was Uncle Henry's favourite sport, so the conversation was animated.

Laurence's friend joined Lucinda by the window. Guy was accustomed to moving in superior circles, so it was no hardship for him to chatter about the gardens and the house.

If Guy was Laurence's chosen best man, he must be one of Laurence's closest friends. She reasoned she was likely to meet him again. He was slim with ash blond hair, a straight carriage, and was dressed in a beautifully fashioned top coat of dark blue with grey pantaloons, a white shirt, and a cravat tied in a complicated style she couldn't name.

He almost outshone Laurence, but not quite. Laurence's close-fitting coat was pale grey with pewter buttons. His pantaloons were a pale beige. A cravat fell on to a white shirt and a grey waistcoat with silver threading.

Throughout the ceremony, when she wanted to avoid meeting anyone else's glance, she looked down at their shoes — his with pewter buckles, and her worn grey slippers peeping from under her dress.

Annie had been adamant that she should not go to her wedding in black, so they had found a dark plum dress in the attic and altered that.

On her wedding day, Annie piled Lucinda's hair high on her head in classical style and arranged curly wisps and ringlets about her face. Lucinda was satisfied with her reflection in the mirror but the shade of the plum dress didn't improve her appearance. It drained her skin of any colour.

Laurence didn't comment when she and her uncle had entered the chapel. He merely nodded to them. Perhaps he didn't even notice what she was wearing. Guy had done his best to bridge the silence as they waited for the clergyman to organise his papers on a side table. Laurence had grown impatient and had gone to hasten him.

Lucinda had visited Castleward, as Laurence had suggested, and lost count of the rooms she toured with the housekeeper. Afterwards they shared tea in a small salon on the ground floor.

When she'd asked Mrs Wilson's opinion whether it was becoming to wear dark plum, instead of black, the housekeeper nodded and smiled.

'Dark plum is very acceptable under the circumstances, ma'am. It's now over three months since your father died. If you lived in London, or attended social events, some might look awry and give you curious glances, but here in the country I don't think it would be wrong if you wore a lighter colour. After all, it's a very special day.'

Mrs Wilson's impression of her future mistress was good. She was well brought up and, from the intelligent questions she asked, it was clear she knew about organising a household. Mrs Wilson reasoned she'd understand any problem in running such a large house very well. She decided she liked her.

'Dark plum is not a colour I would normally choose,' Lucinda admitted, 'but under the circumstances . . . '

'Yes, I imagine green, yellow, pale lavender, or such colours would suit you best, but you naturally have to be careful of social niceties. I think dark plum would be quite fitting.'

Lucinda had nodded, relieved. Her thoughts returned to the present. Guy's face was a caricature of discomfort. He wanted to cheer her.

'I'm sure your father would have loved to be here today,' he said. Lucinda had been thinking the same herself. 'What do you like doing best in your leisure time?' he added.

She replied in a soft, but resolute voice.

'I love books and read all kinds of things. I play the piano, love going for long walks and I enjoyed riding when we still had horses.'

He nodded.

'I've a younger sister and she loves riding too.'

'How long have you known Laurence?'

'Since Oxford. Did you know that Laurence had an older brother? He was killed in the Peninsula Wars.'

Lucinda reflected that was probably the reason Laurence's father had been indifferent to his younger son. He never expected that Laurence would inherit, and even when that happened he had never sought to change his uncaring attitude. It looked like he resented that the inheritance would go to a younger son, whom he didn't know or like very much.

Lucinda shook her head.

'I didn't know he had a brother. I think my father wanted a son, too. Everyone thinks that a son will run an estate better, more effectively, but often I think a daughter might be just as capable if she was raised in the same way, with the same knowledge.' She paused. 'Forgive me if I sound foolish. I know very little about my husband or his friends.'

Guy coloured slightly and he looked uncomfortable. She reached out and touched his arm briefly.

'Please don't feel awkward, Guy. If you're Laurence's friend you also know the circumstances of our marriage.' He nodded. 'Good, then we can always be at ease with each other. Do you have an estate? Are you an older or younger son? Where do you come from?'

He smiled and replied. Lucinda decided she liked him, and Guy decided he liked her, too. Laurence had some luck. She could have turned out to be a harpy, or a money-grabbing nitwit. She was neither. She was bright, intelligent, and well-informed. When he thought about all the young women presented last season in London, even though they were attired perfectly and belonged to the right society, Lucinda would have outshone them all.

When you ignored the 'home-made' dress, she was very pretty, with thick shiny hair and cheerful, intelligent eyes.

Daylight was fading when Uncle Henry came across to say farewell. Laurence thanked him for coming, and he and Lucinda accompanied him outside. Willy and the trap were waiting to take him home.

Lucinda felt a sense of nostalgia when she mused Greystone was no longer her home. She didn't know what the future had in store, but she'd lost her independence at the altar. She was Laurence Ellesporte's property in all but words.

Uncle Henry pecked her cheek and wished her well and hoped to see her again presently at Greystone. She reckoned it was barely three or four miles across the fields. After Laurence left for

London, it would be a pleasant afternoon walk.

When they returned to the sitting-room, Guy was where they left him, sitting in a chair in front of the fire with his legs stretched out in a straight line. He jumped to his feet when they came in.

'That was it, Guy,' Laurence said. 'We'll share a brandy and retire for the night.' He turned to Lucinda. 'You have chosen your rooms?'

Her throat felt dry as she viewed him. It felt like a veiled dismissal.

'Yes. Mrs Wilson tells me they were once your mother's.'

He nodded. His eyes were bland.

'Well, if you want to change something, talk over the technicalities with Mrs Wilson and go ahead. I'm sure you must be tired, so we wish you a good night. I want to consult with the estate manager tomorrow morning. After that, we'll leave and be able to cover most of the distance to London before nightfall.'

Guy looked surprised and he glanced

at Lucinda. She tightened her grip of her cashmere shawl. It was one of her mother's and she loved it. Guy looked uncomfortable as his glance wandered between them.

Lucinda broke the silence.

'It's perfectly all right, Guy. Laurence and I expect nothing quixotic from this marriage. I'm not downhearted.'

She glanced at Laurence.

'Goodnight!' She turned and smiled at him gently. 'Goodnight, Guy!'

She hurried from the room and fled up the majestic staircase. She tried to steady her heartbeat. She didn't know where Laurence's bedroom was, and didn't care.

The ring on her finger felt heavy, and so did her heart. He'd kept his word. They were married and why should she expect him to show any emotion?

She considered the luxury of her spacious bedroom and adjoining dressing-room. Pale jonquil silk covered the walls and a myriad of candles burned brightly from their places on wall-brackets and side-tables. The delicate furniture had a beautiful chestnut sheen, from constant polishing and care.

She viewed the kidney-shaped dressing-table, its empty perfume bottles and other items of prettification.

The writing desk interested her more, and she wondered what she could ever store in the tall commode with its multitude of drawers.

The largest item was the bed with draperies of delicate white silk falling right and left of the headboard. A large Persian carpet in light colours covered the parquet floor. There was also a day bed and some other small tables and chairs.

The adjoining dressing-room was for storing her clothes. At present, it was almost empty. Her simple dresses hung like dark skeletons.

She had never possessed such luxury before and for a moment, she enjoyed the knowledge of possession, but it was bought at a price. She'd agreed to the shell of a marriage.

She doubted that Laurence Ellesporte would ever give much thought to her well-being. He wanted to keep his inheritance. She was just an uncomfortable stipulation in his father's will.

Lucinda was glad to get out of the plum-coloured dress. If she could avoid it, she'd never wear it again. She sat at the dressing-table in her shift and loosened the pins in her hair.

She looked at herself in the mirror, picked up a silver brush, and began to attack it with sweeping strokes. Mrs Wilson had been almost shocked when she discovered that Lucinda had no personal maid.

'That will have to change, my lady. Lady Ellesporte must have one.'

Lucinda was amused. What for? It wasn't likely that she'd attend large social gatherings or give lavish receptions at Castleward.

She remained silent, but admitted that even though it was a waste, her station probably did require such symbols of riches and power.

She didn't know how to go about such things, but she had no doubt that Mrs Wilson did. Some young girl would probably jump at the chance.

Lucinda doused the candles and wondered who'd lit them. She got into bed and settled down among the bedding. She lay awake for a while, and listened to movement on the other side of the wall.

Worlds Apart

Next morning, Laurence was up at dawn. Although he'd never admit it to anyone, he loved the quiet of Castleward at this time of the day.

The servants were starting to light the fires, prepare breakfast, and do the other jobs before family or guests appeared.

Laurence knew how to avoid them, as he scuttled down the back stairs and through the kitchen where the cook handed him a hot cake as he passed. Laurence gave him a smile and the cook winked.

'Just like old times, my lord.'

Until he went to university and for a time afterwards, right up until his brother's death, he'd loved the house and estate dearly.

His father had never shown Laurence much affection. He was an embittered and resentful man. They had never been close, because he looked like his mother, and his mother was the only person who ever stood up to his father. Laurence loved her and he was in his early twenties when she died.

Apart from Guy, she had been the only person he trusted completely. After her death, Castleward lost all its attraction. He inherited a small annuity from his mother and he became one of the Corinthian Set. They were famous for sporting prowess, dress sense and impeccable manners and behaviour. He didn't need his father, and his father didn't want him.

His brother's death had changed all that. His father spent most of the time needling him about his future responsibilities, and telling him how cruelly fate had thwarted his plans. Laurence avoided Castleward and his father as much as possible.

His father did award him a generous allowance when he became heir, but warned him he would not pick up any gambling debts, or pay for any misdemeanours of any kind.

It had still been an enjoyable time, even though his father tried to control him. Now he had also saddled him with an unwanted bride.

Laurence went out to the stables. His favourite horse whinnied in recognition. A sleepy stable boy stumbled in and proceeded to help tack it up.

The boy touched his cap as Laurence set off at a trot across the cobbled yard and the adjoining fields. It felt good to be free of confinement, and he gave the horse its head.

Lengthening its stride, the horse galloped on, its mane flowing in the wind. It was hard to tell whether the horse or its master enjoyed it more.

When they came to the crest of a hill, some miles further on, Laurence reined in the horse, and jumped down. He rode regularly in London, but he missed the empty spaces of the countryside. He studied the familiar surroundings, and had to admit he missed it a lot.

The early morning mist was still clinging to the countryside like a diaphanous gown. The rising sun was still weak, but it would soon spread its warmth across the land.

Since Lord Wentworth had approached him to ask if he was willing to serve his country, freedom like this became very precious. He had given little thought to what would happen if he was discovered. A distant cousin he didn't like, would inherit all this.

Guy was the only person who knew he was working undercover as courier — apart from Lord Wentworth. Guy disapproved of the pre-arranged marriage to Lucinda, even though Laurence had explained he'd saved her from a life of distress.

In the event of his death, the marriage agreement stated that she would re-inherit her old home and some capital to help her make it pay its way. Somehow, he thought she'd manage. He considered it as a commercial transaction, between two estates. Guy saw it differently.

Laurence wondered if he and Lucinda

would get on. She might dislike him — even grow to hate him. Then divorce was the only solution, but socially extremely undesirable. He hoped this marriage where they lived in parallel worlds would work.

She was quite good-looking, if you studied her features carefully. Luckily, she'd agreed to stay in the country so he wouldn't need to introduce his wife to society in London.

When he clattered back into the yard, the servants were busy. He handed the reins to the waiting stable boy, and after a soft clap to the horse's hindquarters and some soft words in its ear, he went back into the house.

Guy was in the breakfast-room. He joined him and took his place at the head of the table.

'Where have you been?' He eyed his friend's attire. 'Riding at this time of the day?'

'Yes, out to Towning Hill and back via Hallows Wood.'

'You should have told me,' Guy replied, munching some beef. 'I would have come with you.'

'I wanted to be on my own.'

Guy wasn't bothered by his answer. The two men knew each other like brothers.

Laurence helped himself to a generous portion of ham and indicated to a servant hovering in the background to fill his cup.

The two men talked about the political situation. A London paper a few days old had arrived that morning. Sharing the pages, they commented now and again on an article.

When Lucinda arrived, they rose to their feet. She was wearing one of the drab grey dresses she'd made with Annie's help.

'Good morning!' She took a seat.

They both echoed her words. Guy smiled across the table.

'I hope you slept well?'

'Thank you, very well. You, too?'

'I always do when I come here. I think it has something to do with the country air.'

Laurence rose.

'I'm going to check with the estate manager, change, and then we'll be ready to leave. We'll stop somewhere along the way this evening and drive into London early tomorrow morning.'

Guy nodded while buttering a piece of bread.

Laurence gave Lucinda his attention.

'I hope you'll feel well in Castleward. You have a free hand to do as you see fit.' He paused for the slightest moment. 'I hope you'll not mind when I remark that I think it would be a good idea if you get a trained seamstress to make you some dresses. You're still in mourning, but there is no reason why you should look shabbier than one of the servants. Always remember that you're Lady Ellesporte.'

He bent quickly and brushed his lips across the back of her hand.

'We won't see each other again before I leave. I hope to find you in good health next time we meet.'

Lucinda flushed but she answered

with equilibrium.

'Thank you. I'll do as you suggest. I hope you have a good journey.' Guy looked abashed.

'I beg your pardon for being an unwilling eavesdropper.

She hurried to reassure him.

'It's all right, Guy. He's perfectly right. I know my clothes are not up to scratch. I had no money to buy any attractive mourning apparel.

'I had to use clothes my mother wore for a relative's death twenty years ago. Annie, my old nurse, and I did our best, but now I must try to present a better picture. Mrs Wilson suggests I employ a lady's maid, too, so I hope that my appearance will please him better next time we meet.'

He smiled at her again.

'I think it makes no difference. Anyone with any sense will see the kind of person you are, not what you're wearing.'

She laughed.

'Do you realise that you're saying that Laurence doesn't have much sense?'

They looked at each other and started laughing. Laurence, crossing the hallway, felt annoyed that his friend had made his wife laugh. Then he realised that he'd never even given her the slightest reason to smile.

★ ★ ★

A few hours later, Lucinda watched from her bedroom as the coach drove down the curved driveway.

Both men were inside. Laurence's valet sat on top at the rear, and a groom and the driver were in front. A beautifully matched pair of chestnut horses pulled the vehicle. It looked impressive and was well sprung.

Lucinda knew people who visited London regularly said road conditions were improving, but a long journey was more comfortable in such a vehicle than by stage, or even the post chaise. She heaved a sign of relief and turned her thoughts to other things.

Lady of the House

Lounging into the comfortable upholstery, Guy stuck his top-boots out across
the divide between them and contem-
plated his friend. Laurence was looking
out of the window at the passing scenery.

'Your ancestors chose a delightful
place to build,' Guy commented.

'Yes, I'm very attached to it. Especially now my father reigns no more.'

'I always admired the way you
swallowed your spleen. He was often in
dudgeon when you met, wasn't he?'

Laurence adjusted his cravat.

'That's why I kept out of his way as
much as I could.'

Guy took a pinch of snuff.

'I never understood it, old boy. After
all, you were never a ramshackle chap,
or in Dun territory. He was never
forced to help you out.'

Laurence squared his shoulders.

'I took care never to be on the rocks. I didn't give him more ammunition to fire than he had already.'

'If he'd known that they've asked you to serve your country, he might have changed his attitude.'

'I doubt it. If I wore a uniform and got myself killed in some outlandish spot no-one has ever heard of, it would have pleased him more.'

Guy could tell his friend needed diversion from such thoughts.

'I like Lucinda.'

'Do you? I don't know enough about her to care one way or the other. The estates are joined — that was the aim. My father was an odd fish, but he excelled at keeping the estates in good order and increasing his wealth.

'It's strange that I never met her before,' he added, 'but I'm years older and I seldom rode in that direction. I never attended local assemblies, either, so we never crossed paths. I explained what my old man put in the agreement, didn't I?'

'Yes. It must be darned difficult for Lucinda. You're practically a stranger, she had no choice in the matter, and she has no helpful relations. Her uncle is more interested in Mesopotamia than in his niece. It must have been a great shock when she found out.'

Laurence shrugged.

'From what I've seen of Greystone, her life from now on will be a great deal more comfortable than it was before. At least her uncle was caring enough to make sure the marriage agreement was all it should be. She's not completely neglected.'

Laurence shifted and Guy persisted.

'I'm sure she'll do her best, now that she realises she has no other choice. She's never had a London season, has she? I think you don't realise that she's a very pleasant, intelligent girl. She's discreet, honest, she talks sense, and she's a good listener. She's also well read, and knows a lot about history. Apparently, she even had a French governess once, for a couple of years.'

Laurence smiled.

'You sound like one of those hen-witted women in a London drawing-room weighing up a new arrival. Oh, good heavens, I hope she's not a bluestocking, is she? I don't suppose we'll see much of each other, but I don't aspire to discussing Aristotle or the latest archaeological finds with my wife every time we meet.'

'Well, if I ever marry, I'd like someone like Lucinda. She's not a feather-head. You should be grateful. You have no reason to feel ashamed of your new wife.'

'I wasn't aware that I said that I am.' He eyed his friend. Guy wasn't usually quick to praise any woman. The new faces who appeared every season didn't interest him. He had loved a girl, long ago, but she died tragically of consumption, and he'd been inconsolable for years afterwards. Anyone new was always found wanting. He wasn't as wealthy, but Guy's estate was prosperous, he had pleasant features, and he was a good friend.

'I just hope that she represents the Ellesporte name properly,' Laurence remarked.

Guy turned his head and looked out of the window.

'Well, she's bound to be a resounding success with the all-encompassing help and support she gets from you,' he declared.

Laurence laughed loudly.

'You think I ought to find her some help?' he countered.

Guy viewed his friend.

'Yes, I do. She needs someone to support and help her to adjust to the new situation. Don't you have someone in the family, someone who knows all the ropes?'

Laurence's brow crinkled.

'This marriage is getting more complicated than I expected,' he muttered, then was silent for a few seconds. 'Wait! I've just remembered someone — my father's sister, Aunt Eliza. She's full of spirit.

'She rebelled and married Walter

Thursby, a man without title or money. What he did have, he spent on clothes and entertaining. As long as he lived, they led a very interesting life. My father ignored them whenever he could.

'Thursby died a couple of years ago, and because she was purse-pinched, my aunt retired to a small cottage outside Brighton. I visited her not so long ago and cautiously offered a small additional annuity. But she wouldn't accept, and insisted she was managing. She always made me laugh whenever we met because she's very forthright and honest, and often told me not to act so puffed-up.'

'Then she's the solution! She might be glad to visit Castleward, because she'd save money and she would think she's doing you a favour, so she won't feel beholden. It sounds like she has enough experience of society to help Lucinda.'

Laurence tapped the roof of the carriage.

'Tell you what, we'll visit her on the

way and ask her. We'll have to stop overnight somewhere anyway. If we go to Brighton, we can travel on to London from there tomorrow and still be there by early afternoon if we have a good run.'

Laurence stuck his head out of the window.

'Head for Brighton instead of London!' he shouted.

'Yes, my lord. They have Cleveland Bays at the Crown. That's our next stop. They'll be fresh, and perhaps with one more change, we'll be in Brighton by five o'clock.'

Satisfied, Laurence leaned back into the upholstery.

'If you persuade your aunt, remember to phrase your letter to Lucinda carefully when you explain who she is,' Guy remarked. 'Tell her she's a relative who wants to see Castleward again. It won't help Lucinda if she thinks your aunt is coming to supervise her. That will just make her more nervous.'

Laurence looked at his friend in

surprise and chuckled.

'I swear it!'

* * *

After the men left, Lucinda felt wary for the first couple of weeks, and on guard. Mrs Wilson ran the household on oiled wheels, and apart from approving menus, listening to the housekeeper's plans for the upkeep, checking the household linens for repair, and hearing which vegetables and fruits were being bottled at present, she had little to occupy her time.

At Greystone Lucinda had always been busy. For a while, she filled in the time with exploring the house, going for walks through the landscaped gardens or the nearby countryside, and reading.

When one morning the butler came to enquire if she'd receive Mrs Stevenson and her daughter Judith, Lucinda almost clapped her hands in delight.

Once her guests were seated, Mrs Stevenson spoke.

'The news has spread, Lucinda. It was a great surprise because no-one realised that you knew Lord Ellesporte. When we heard of the forthcoming nuptials, we wanted to be there on your wedding day. I hope you did not mind? Mr Stevenson and I offer you our heartfelt congratulations, my dear. We are all delighted for you.'

'Thank you, dear Mrs Stevenson. I'm was delighted to see some old friends.' Lucinda got up and pressed the button on the side of the mantelpiece.

The butler appeared again.

'Some refreshments for the ladies, please, William.' He bowed and withdrew.

Judith tittered and pressed her hand over her mouth.

'Forgive me, Lucinda. It seems so strange to know you're Lady Ellesporte, and see you command your new butler.'

Lucinda laughed softly.

'Yes. I am still getting used to it myself.'

'Is your husband at home?' Mrs

Stevenson asked. 'Perhaps he's out attending to the estate?'

'No, he had to travel to London on urgent business and I don't know when he'll return.'

'It's understandable,' Mrs Stevenson remarked, nodding. 'Someone with such extensive properties has great responsibility, and must pay attention to many things. London is the centre of all business and legal matters. I expect we will see you there soon, too?'

William came in with a silver tray. On it was a silver teapot, milk jug, sugar bowl, fine china cups and saucers, and a plate of small cakes. Lucinda busied herself with pouring tea for her guests.

'I don't plan to visit London in the near future. I am happiest here,' she remarked.

'But you must, Lucinda!' Judith blurted out. 'There is so much to see and do. You will enjoy it, I'm sure.'

Judith was still a little saddened that Lucinda had not told her she was going to be betrothed to Laurence Ellesporte.

Mama believed both families had agreed on the marriage long ago, but a definite date had never been fixed.

Perhaps Lucinda's father planned it to take place when she became of age, or after a London season. His death had probably accelerated intentions, and led to Lucinda's hasty marriage.

Lucinda redirected the conversation.

'Perhaps I will, one day. At present, I must attend to my duties here. There is much to do and supervise.' She would have to think of a plausible reason why she had not told Judith earlier about a 'secret' betrothal.

Mrs Stevenson nodded.

'Of course. The vicar and his wife mentioned that they intend to call soon, and I've no doubt others will also pay their respects, now that you're Lady Ellesporte.'

Lucinda smiled.

'Yes, I expect many people who barely gave Lucinda Harting the time of day before, will now want to bring themselves to the notice of Lady Ellesporte.'

Mrs Stevenson took a sip of tea from the gold-rimmed teacup.

'Ah well! Yes, perhaps some will try to flatter you because of your position, but you're much too sensible not to discern between flattery and honest friendship.'

'I hope so. One thing is certain — the Stevensons always gave me friendship and welcomed me to their home. You will always be very welcome here.

'I hope Judith and I remain great friends. There are some delightful walks nearby, the library contains some very interesting books, and there are capital horses in the stable that the groom assures me are perfect for young ladies.'

Judith eyes sparkled.

'Oh, that will be fun. You're lucky, Lucinda, but you deserve it. I'll be so happy if we remain good friends and we can visit each other, provided Mama allows me, of course.'

Mrs Stevenson nodded indulgently.

'As long as you don't outstay your welcome.'

'Judith and I are the very best of

friends,' Lucinda said reassuringly, 'and I hope that will never change. Would you like to tour the house?' Her eyes sparkled. 'Then you'll have a head start on anyone else who calls.'

Mrs Stevenson laughed.

'Lucinda! I'm glad that marriage has not changed your sense of humour one little bit.'

'Mrs Wilson, our housekeeper, will be delighted to show you around. She's a very friendly and capable woman.' Lucinda pressed the bell again and asked William to find Mrs Wilson.

Mrs Wilson came. If she was doing something more important, she didn't show it. They made a quick tour of Castleward. Mrs Wilson explained the history of the building and mother and daughter were impressed. Both of them declared they had never viewed a house that was more elegant, or more comfortable. Tour over, they took their leave, and Judith promised to call again very soon.

Help is at Hand

Lucinda knew she had to improve on her appearance and wondered how to do so. She was unwilling to turn to Mrs Wilson again. Too much dependency was bad. She needed a good dressmaker, but where could she find one?

The last time she'd had a new dress made for the assembly dances was two years ago — a delightful gown of white sarsnet with a pale blue body, and long sleeves that buttoned tightly around her wrists. The dressmaker came to Greystone to measure and make suggestions.

Lucinda had loved that dress — until someone accidentally tipped red punch over it and it was ruined. Lucinda had no idea where the seamstress came from. Perhaps Annie knew.

Several days later she was in the kitchen garden when a maid came to tell her a lady had called and was waiting in the drawing-room. Puzzled, Lucinda went back inside.

A middle-aged woman in a travelling coat and wearing a large lilac turban decorated with some very large feathers was sitting near the fireplace looking through an old magazine that Lucinda had unearthed in the library.

She glanced up when Lucinda came in.

'Heavens, this is years out of date,' she remarked.

'Yes, I know. I've been wondering how to arrange for a new subscription. Good morning, ma'am. Can I help you? I do not think we have met before, have we?'

Aunt Eliza considered her for a moment. She was not a raving beauty, never would be, even with some decent clothes and good hairstyle, but she had a winning smile and she was pretty. The girl possessed something that would outlast physical beauty. She had poise and dignity.

'No, we haven't. I am Laurence's

aunt. Call me Eliza. Don't dare call me Aunt Eliza. I won't like that at all.'

Lucinda's heart beat faster at this unexpected development.

'Then please make yourself comfortable, and I'll send for refreshments. You must be tired after your journey.'

Eliza took off her turban and placed it next to her coat on a nearby chair.

The butler appeared.

'William, will you please arrange tea and something appropriate to eat,' Lucinda asked him. She indicated the items on the chair. 'Ask Mrs Wilson to prepare our best guest room and have those things taken upstairs with any luggage as soon as the room is ready.'

With a dignified bow, William withdrew.

'He wasn't here last time I was in Castleward,' Eliza remarked, 'but that's not surprising, it was years ago. Didn't Laurence warn you I was coming?'

Lucinda shook her head.

'The post is always tardy. Perhaps a note is still on the way. Anyway,

Laurence knows it is unnecessary to warn me that his aunt, who grew up in Castleward, is visiting. You are welcome here whenever you wish to come.'

Eliza listened carefully to Lucinda's declaration.

'Laurence's father wouldn't have agreed with you.'

'Why ever not?' Lucinda said, startled.

'It's a long story, and I'll tell you about it one day.' Eliza's instincts told her that this young woman was someone who didn't judge, or give counsel, unless it was asked of her.

'Castleward looks in top form. Changed from when I was last here. My brother was a penny-pincher and he begrudged every shilling that didn't bring a quick return. He invested in the estates, but not in the living quarters.'

The tea arrived and Lucinda poured her a welcome cup.

'Laurence is different,' Eliza continued. 'He realises that there's no point in having money unless you show others you enjoy it. I don't mean he throws money around but he knows what he's doing and he gets enjoyment from his possessions.'

'Yes, I think that is true.' Lucinda paused. 'Our marriage must be a surprise.'

'Oh, not really. He's old enough and he's responsible for producing an heir for Castleward. It's no good deciding to marry when a man is too old.'

Lucinda coloured and looked down for a moment — something Eliza didn't miss. She viewed her closely.

'I see you wear blacks because your father died recently, but you can afford more flattering clothes now.'

Lucinda flinched inwardly at the remark, but her mind lightened with the possibility of involving Eliza in her dilemma. She already liked Eliza. She was forthright and she knew something about fashion — anyone could tell that by just looking at her beautiful silk dress and the rows of dancing pearls on her chest.

She was no youngster, but she still

knew how to make the best of herself. She had an upright carriage and a good figure.

'Laurence told me to get some suitable dresses,' Lucinda explained, 'but I don't know where or how. I didn't think it was right to involve the housekeeper. Someone I know, the mother of a good friend, might have helped, but I thought she might even find it a strange request. I've been wondering how to solve the problem without looking like a nincompoop.'

'Then we will solve it together. The nearest town to this place is Winchester. There used to be a couple of good dressmakers, and I don't suppose that has changed.

'Where there are dressmakers, there are hats, shoes, and gloves. I'll enjoy helping to rig you out, and we don't need to worry about the cost, either.

'How long have you been in blacks?' she added. 'It's a pity that you're not out of mourning because black doesn't suit your pale complexion, but you can start to wear slightly lighter colours like grey, lavender, or violet.'

'It's over five months since my dear papa died. I'd love to wear some other colour. Black is so dismal. I still miss my father and a part of me will always mourn him, but I think mourning has more to do with missing someone than what colour you're wearing, don't you?'

'You're quite right, child. My husband hated me in black when he lived and he'd have encouraged me to ignore protocol after he died, but sometimes you have to knuckle under or be an outcast.' She paused. 'Six months is long enough for deep mourning. By the end of the year you'll be able to wear bright colours again.'

Lucinda's eyes sparkled.

'Choosing new clothes will be fun. I hope you'll also help me find a lady's maid? Mrs Wilson insists I should have one and I don't know where to start.' She smiled at Eliza. 'I'm so glad you've come, Eliza.'

The older woman viewed her kindly.

'And I'm glad I've come, child. I was curious about the woman Laurence has chosen, but you'll do very well.'

'I don't suppose that Laurence has explained why he married me? That is a long story, too.' She lifted the silver teapot. 'More tea? Then you must rest after the journey and we will talk again later. I'm so glad that I don't have to sit at the head of that long table and eat on my own. I've even started wondering who I could persuade to join me.'

Eliza's brows arched and she laughed.

Lucinda viewed her. Eliza's voice was full of humour and honesty. Lucinda knew that in the world of the nobility, many people avoided honesty because it led to further blunders. They preferred to ingratiate themselves with falsehoods than to be truthful and perhaps end up as an outcast.

A Day to Remember

A week later Eliza was recovered and ready to take Lucinda to buy some new clothes.

'Your present dresses are only fit for bottling blackcurrants. We'll go to Winchester and stay a day or two because we have plenty to do. We must visit the dressmaker, the milliner, the hosier, the linen draper, and the haberdasher. You will need at least three day dresses, two evening dresses, a redingote, a couple of spencer jackets, hats, gloves, undergarments, slippers, half-boots . . .'

Lucinda covered her ears.

'Stop, Eliza, stop! Why so many dresses? I'll be able to wear more cheerful colours by the end of the year. Any such attire will perhaps hang ignored in the wardrobe. Anyway, Laurence might not approve of spending so much money.'

'Don't worry about Laurence. He's

not stupid. He knows a wife costs money. You need to dress properly, Lucinda. Forget about the past. You are Lady Ellesporte. You choose carefully and will always be able to wear them as day dresses. We'll stay at the Red Hen, if it's still there. They have quiet bedrooms overlooking the back yard, and they always had a good kitchen. Have you ever been to Winchester?'

'Yes, a couple of times, with my father and once to the assembly with Mrs Stevenson. I enjoyed it all very much. There was so much activity and bustle.'

Eliza decided Lucinda must visit London. Laurence said she loved the countryside and had no interest in big cities. She wasn't sure about that any more. Lucinda was resolute with a bubbly personality. She had a winning smile and genteel manners. She was beginning to wonder how well, if at all, Laurence knew his wife.

★ ★ ★

The journey took most of the morning and Eliza had to stop Lucinda sticking her head out of the window once they reached the edge of the town.

The Red Hen was on a main thoroughway, but their rooms provided privacy and peace. One of the inn's maids had been told to help the illustrious guests.

Eliza enquired of the innkeeper's wife where they could find the best seamstress.

They went for a short walk that afternoon, and Lucinda noticed her dress was extremely shabby in comparison to that of the young women they passed. Only the tight-fitting dark blue spencer with its gold togging and decorative buttons, bought last winter, helped conceal the bad quality of the dress beneath.

On their return to the inn, they shared their evening meal, played cards for a while and then retired early. Eliza warned her they would need all their energy for tomorrow.

After breakfast, they went to the recommended seamstress. When Lucinda explained who she was and that she needed several garments, the seamstress called for refreshments.

For an hour or so, Lucinda studied the drawings in Ackerman's, and talked with Eliza and the seamstress about the ones she admired. The seamstress suggested slight changes now and then, ones that she thought would complement Lucinda. Eliza was pleased and relieved to notice that Lucinda had good taste.

One of the assistants in the shop attended to them when the dressmaker was called elsewhere. She was a very sensible girl, neatly dressed, her hair nicely arranged, and she had a pleasant voice. She made prudent suggestions, and recommended where to find the various shops.

The materials and accessories for six dresses, a redingote, undergarments, and spencers took some time to acquire. Eliza instructed the shopkeepers to send the bills to Lord Ellesporte and to deliver the ware to the seamstress immediately.

Tired but satisfied, they returned to the Red Hen. Eliza declared she must rest, otherwise she would not be fit to go down to dinner.

Lucinda was also happy to sit and watch the comings and goings in the yard down below. She wondered if they would have time to do anything else apart from shopping for clothes. As much as she loved that, she hoped to visit some bookshops, and the cathedral if there was time.

★ ★ ★

Next morning, they set out with not quite as much élan to find accessories. Eliza was in command. They bought stockings and gloves, and then went to the milliner, to choose some bonnets.

Looking out of the window, Lucinda saw the young girl from the seamstress shop was passing. She smiled at Lucinda who was trying on one of the bonnets.

She nodded vigorously. Lucinda picked up another and turned to the window. The girl shook her head just as vigorously. Lucinda nodded and waved as the girl left again. She turned to Eliza.

'Eliza, I was just thinking . . . '

'You were thinking that girl might be suitable to be your maid.'

'Yes. How did you guess?'

'Because I had the same thought myself. She knows about fashion and she'd know how to look after your clothes. She's neat and her hair is dressed fashionably. She's also polite and well-mannered. I think she'd love to be lady's maid at Castleward. Did you know that many seamstresses work twelve to fifteen hours a day for a pittance?'

Lucinda nodded.

'The vicar's wife told me about such things. I have a bad conscience.'

Eliza shrugged.

'It's the way of the world. More people are moving from the country to the town, and work is scarce. Employers have the upper hand. I hear that lots of people work in big factories under appalling conditions. Sometimes I wonder why they don't rebel like the people did in France. There, the nobility paid the price for greed and not caring.'

'Will that happen here, Eliza?' Lucinda exclaimed with a shocked expression.

'I hope not. The English are different in their way of thinking, and there are people in parliament who try to improve things and lessen the injustices, but it's an uphill fight. Come, we are not finished yet.'

'Will the seamstress be angry when we tempt one of her workers away?'

Eliza gave her a haughty look.

'Not if she had her eye on business. Anyone who can report that Lady Ellesporte is one of her customers is likely to attract other customers. She wants to keep your custom more than one of her workers. There are dozens of other girls just waiting for the chance to be this girl's replacement.'

After a refreshing hot chocolate in a nearby inn, they went to buy some half-boots. Lucinda had no qualms about buying three pairs, in brown, pale grey and black. She reasoned that she could wear those even when the mourning period was over. She'd always need half-boots. They added some light slippers for indoors and were happy with the morning's work.

They called at the seamstress on their way back to the Red Hen. She assured them that the redingote and one of the day dresses would be delivered to the inn that afternoon, and the others would be in Castleward within the week.

Eliza cornered the young girl while Lucinda engaged the seamstress in conversation. Lucinda could see from the way that Molly's eyes lit up that she'd be happy to come to Castleward.

Eliza gave in to Lucinda's plea to linger at a book shop on the way back to the inn. Lucinda found her a quiet corner with a magazine and went in search of something new to read.

The library at Castleward contained

hundreds of books, most of which dealt with politics, religion, botany, estate management, law, and gardening. She needed entertainment, and bought two novels that were the current rage.

Satisfied, she found Eliza again. The afternoon was well advanced by the time they reached the Red Hen.

Soon after they'd finished their supper in their private parlour, Molly arrived with a large package and a small cloth bag. She had come to stay. Molly's features were a mixture of uncertainty and bright anticipation. Eliza took charge.

'Come in, child. Put the parcel down and take off your cloak. You can help your future mistress into her new clothes.'

Glad to have something to do, to cover her uncertainty, Molly obeyed. They all retired to Lucinda's bedroom where Lucinda was transformed from an unassuming young woman to someone who caught the eye.

With heightened colour, Lucinda had to admit that fashionable clothes made a great difference. The day dress was of grey batiste, with a high waistline, square neckline, and long sleeves. It was decorated on the hemline, neck-edging, and sleeves with a little embroidered trimming in a darker shade of grey. It flattered her slim figure and the hem swished as she moved.

Eliza nodded.

'It suits you, Lucinda. It fits properly and, because the decoration is under-stated, it is chic. It makes a world of difference. You have a pretty face, but even a pretty face needs some comple-mentary pretty clothes.'

'Oh, yes, miss,' Molly added. 'You look beautiful.'

Lucinda twirled, and nodded.

'I love it.'

Molly held out the redingote and Lucinda slipped into it. It fitted perfectly. It was dark violet with cord trimmings, banded at the high waist, and with sturdy front fastening. The other two nodded their approval. Lucinda felt she looked like Lady

Ellesporte, at last.

'With that new poke bonnet in grey, it will look perfect,' Eliza remarked. She turned to Molly. 'You can help your mistress de-robe and I'll instruct the innkeeper to send up a truckle bed. You'll sleep in this room tonight.

'When we reach Castleward tomorrow, the housekeeper will decide where you will sleep. You'll share your meals with the upper servants, and Mrs Wilson the housekeeper will explain exactly what your duties are.

'Yes, madam. Thank you. I'll do my very best to be a worthy maid.'

Eliza nodded approvingly.

'Don't thank me, child. Lady Ellesporte is your mistress. We both thought you could be a good lady's maid.' She turned and left the other two alone.

Molly helped Lucinda undress and when Lucinda sat down at the makepiece dressing-table, she picked up the hair brush and proceeded to brush Lucinda's thick shiny hair.

Unexpected Arrival

Next morning, Molly sat next to Lucinda in the carriage, and she could hardly contain her excitement. She explained that she had never been in a real carriage before. Eliza and Lucinda viewed her indulgently.

They stopped for refreshments along the way, and Molly got them immediate attention and the best that the inn had to offer. The driver and groom were busy overseeing the changing of the horses, so Molly undertook the task of getting refreshments.

They reached Castleward that afternoon and Molly's eyes widened when they drove up the long tree-lined drive and halted in front of the steps leading up to the portico. The butler was already waiting at the doorway and bowed slightly.

'Welcome back, my lady, Mrs Thursby.'

He looked at Molly.

'This is Molly, my new maid,' Lucinda explained. 'Please inform Mrs Wilson that she needs a room, and suitable dress.'

He studied Molly more carefully.

'Certainly, my lady. Follow me,' he added, addressing Molly, 'and wait while I accompany the ladies to the drawing-room.' He turned back to Lucinda and Eliza. 'I ordered tea when I saw the carriage entering the drive. It's waiting for you in the green salon. I hope that meets with your approval, my lady?'

Removing her bonnet, Lucinda agreed willingly.

'Thank you, William. Go with William, Molly. I'll see you later.'

Molly bobbed a curtsey.

'Yes, my lady.' She waited while William handed their travelling attire to another servant. He proceeded Lucinda and Eliza into the drawing-room, then closed the door and left.

Eliza sat down and smiled.

'She'll do, Lucinda. She's adaptable,

and has no airs, although I'm sure she realises that her position is superior to the other servants. They will keep their distance till they know her, but that's not a bad thing. She has to learn to hold her tongue and ignore the tittle-tattle in the servants' pantry.'

Lucinda patted her hair.

'Well, she manages my hair beautifully. I would never have managed this style on my own.'

Eliza smiled. Lucinda reached forward and poured them tea.

'Our trip to Winchester was worthwhile. You are now very smart. I think that when you no longer need to wear blacks that you'll take London by storm.'

Lucinda took a sip of tea.

'I don't think I'll ever take London by storm, Eliza. Laurence and I have an agreement. He intends to live his life in London, and I will live here, as before.'

Eliza's eyes widened in surprise.

'What do you mean?'

Lucinda explained how their marriage

had come about and why Laurence and she didn't intend to change their life-styles.

Eliza spluttered.

'My brother arranged a marriage for a girl he'd never met? That is contemptible! So, it isn't a love match?'

Lucinda shook her head.

'I met Laurence for the first time on the day he told me what our fathers had arranged. I was shocked at the time, but adjoining estates are often joined by marriage. My father was in great debt to your brother, so it wasn't difficult for Papa to agree. He thought he was securing my future by doing so.'

Eliza nodded.

'Such arrangements are settled because men have all the say. I refused to be bargained off, and all my family, apart from Laurence, practically ignored me completely thereafter. I don't regret it, though. My husband and I had a wonderful marriage and a wonderful life together.'

Lucinda gave a tremulous smile.

'Then you were lucky. I had no choice. I know of no-one else who would have married me. Even if I sold Greystone, I'd have still be indebted to Castleward. I'd be a pauper with no way of earning a living.'

Eliza reached out and covered her hand.

'It is a pity, but Laurence is a good man, Lucinda. I don't think you need to fear him.'

'No, I don't fear him,' she replied with glistening eyes. 'He has treated me fairly and without animosity. I think he's a very polite man, who was also trapped by circumstances. In your brother's will, if he refused to marry me he'd be disinherited.'

'Good heavens!' Eliza blurted out, her cup suspended in mid-air. 'My brother was a mutton head!'

Lucinda laughed weakly.

'I don't mind. I've never been to London. Lady Stevenson and her daughter Judith, who is a very good friend of mine, have and told me all about it. It sounds like you barely have time to catch your breath, because of all the various dances, assemblies, entertainments, and dinners. I was always content with our local assembly every fortnight. The waltz was allowed last time. My father allowed me to go because Lady Stevenson acted as my chaperone. I'm not sure if I can attend now that I'm Lady Ellesporte.'

'Lord preserve me! Of course you may. I imagine that the locals will queue up to dance with Lady Ellesporte. As a married woman you don't need a chaperone any more, although it is advisable to go with someone else like this Lady Stevenson you mention. You must invite her to tea, so that I can make her acquaintance. Tell me about the family.'

'They are very respectable. Mr Stevenson is a Justice of the Peace. They own a small estate. Mrs Stevenson is the youngest daughter of Lord Marlow.'

'Marlow? Can't say I've ever heard the name. Perhaps he's a member of the lesser nobility, and doesn't mix with the London set.'

'I think he comes from the north. Mrs Stevenson met her husband when she was presented, and that's why she is eager for Judith to have a season, too. She has a married sister who has a town house in London, and the family is well connected.

'Judith's presentation at court is already arranged. Mrs Stevenson's sister knows someone who has put her name forward.' She paused for a moment.

'Would it be wrong of me to parade my new clothes in front of Mrs Stevenson and Judith? I have never had such fine things before.'

'No, of course not. They are befitting to your new status. Your friend's name is unknown to me, but most of the people in London are not worth knowing anyway. The interesting people are often the ones on the edge of society.'

★ ★ ★

Two days later, Mrs Stevenson and Judith called, and met Eliza. When they saw Lucinda in her new dress and a matching ribbon threaded through her curls to keep them in order, they looked suitably impressed.

'Oh, you look quite the thing, Lucinda!' Judith exclaimed. 'Who managed to braid your hair and put it up in such an attractive way?'

Lucinda laughed.

'Yes, clothes make a difference, don't they? Come with me and see the other things we've bought, Judith. They arrived this morning and I haven't tried them on yet. Aunt Eliza helped me choose everything, and she has excellent taste.'

Judith clapped her hands in glee.

'Oh, yes. I'd love that.' She hugged her friend. 'I'm so happy for you, Lucinda. You deserve the best of everything. I've always thought so.'

The two younger women exited, and left the two older ladies to enjoy some tea and some freshly made madeleines. Eliza found she had gone to boarding school with a friend of Mrs Stevenson, so the ice was broken.

Lucinda and Judith returned to tell them how well the clothes fitted. Judith was very enthusiastic.

'When Lucinda is out of mourning she'll be able to wear colours that will suit her colouring even better, but these clothes are already beautifully made and show her for what she is, a lady.'

The sound of heavy footsteps interrupted their conversation and the door flew open to admit Laurence and Guy. They looked at the gathering in surprise.

Eliza reacted quickest.

'Laurence, were we warned of your arrival?

Laurence was wearing beige buckskin pantaloons buttoned down the side, a claw hammer coat of bottle green, and black riding boots with tan top edgings and small tassels. Following the two men, William hastily took their hats and gloves.

'No, Eliza. Did I need to warn you? I'm afraid it didn't occur to me.'

Eliza was never lost for words.

'Then you must be passing through? Where are you going to, or coming from?'

Laurence crossed the room and bent his head over Lucinda's hand.

'Good morning, Lucinda. I hope you're well.' He viewed her carefully and noticed her improved appearance, but didn't comment.

Guy did.

'Good morning, Lady Ellesporte. May I remark how well you look!' His eyes twinkled.

Laurence turned to Lucinda's guests.

'I see we have visitors.'

Lucinda hurried to introduce them.

'This is Mrs Stevenson and her daughter Judith. Mr Stevenson is Justice of the Peace and has an estate on the other side of Greystone. The Stevenson family has always been very kind to me.'

Laurence bowed easily.

'Then I have every reason to be grateful to them. It's a pleasure to meet you, ma'am!' He paused for a moment while he considered them more closely. 'I think we've met before, haven't we? At Lord Taylor's concert a few months ago.'

Mrs Stevenson studied his handsome features.

'Yes, my lord,' she said. 'You're right. We were not formally introduced, but we did attend the concert and enjoyed it very much, didn't we, Judith?'

'Yes, Mama. It was a delightful evening.'

Laurence nodded.

'Someone mentioned that you came from near Castleward. That's why I recall seeing you there.' He turned to Guy. 'This is my friend, Mr Guy Mannering.'

Guy bowed.

'Your servant, Mrs Stevenson, Miss Stevenson.'

Guy viewed Judith longer than necessary and she held his glance for a moment, before she looked down and fiddled with her pink reticule. Lucinda recalled that blondes were all the rage in London.

'Judith is to be presented this season,'

Lucinda added quickly, 'and she's looking forward to it very much.'

Judith looked across to her friend and her blue eyes twinkled.

'Then I expect we'll have the pleasure of seeing you in London soon, Miss Stevenson,' Guy declared.

Judith nodded and viewed the two men innocently. She had creamy skin, a rosebud mouth, and a slender figure.

Laurence noted Guy's interest in the chit — understandably — the girl was very pretty. The pale pink dress she was wearing completed an impression of a china shepherdess.

He was also pleased about how a decent dress improved Lucinda's appearance by leaps and bounds. She should wear bolder colours, but a well-made dress already made an immense difference. He addressed Mrs Stevenson.

'It would give us great pleasure if you and your family would come to dinner tomorrow evening.'

Flustered, Mrs Stevenson replied quickly. 'It will be our pleasure, Lord

Ellesporte. Thank you, we will come.'
She turned to her daughter and tapped
her on her arm.

'Judith, we shall leave now. Lord and
Lady Ellesporte need to catch up on
their news.' She rose and Judith followed immediately without protest.

Guy proceeded them to open the
door. He smiled at them both and
bowed slightly before they departed.

'They seem like decent people,'
Laurence commented.

'They are,' Eliza replied. 'The girl is
still too clinging and unsophisticated,
but a season in London will make all
the difference. Her mother is a sensible
woman, and I expect her parents are
hoping she'll make a good match, I
don't think they'll push the girl into an
unsuitable marriage, and she's pretty
enough to do well.'

Lucinda looked down hastily. She
knew Eliza didn't intend to be hurtful
but the reference to being pushed into
an unsuitable marriage made her feel ill
at ease.

Laurence sat down in a chair next to the fireplace and indicated that Guy should do the same.

'Anything important happened since I was last here? I don't mean about the estate, the agent will tell me all about that, I mean anything personal.'

Eliza didn't wait for Lucinda.

'As you can tell, we've been shopping in Winchester for a couple of outfits for Lucinda.'

Laurence viewed his wife through his pince-nez.

'Yes, I already noticed.'

Eliza prattled on.

'We have also engaged a lady's maid — a country girl with no cobwebs in her head. She knows exactly what's expected of her. I suspect your housekeeper has given her the necessary instructions about her position and her duties.'

'And I hope you're comfortable, Eliza?'

'Thank you, yes. Lucinda has done everything to make me welcome. The staff is very well trained. I am enjoying my stay.'

'Good!' He rose. 'I'll leave you now. We only intended to stay overnight but we'll postpone our departure, now the Stevensons are coming to dinner tomorrow. It doesn't make any difference to you does it, Guy?'

'No, not at all. There is nothing waiting for me in London. There's a fight at the end of the week which I want to attend, but we will be back before then.'

'Who's fighting?'

'Jud Bolton versus Chad Jaynes.'

'I'll join you. I saw Jaynes fighting Walter Tillingsford not so long ago. It was a good set-to.' He got up and strolled towards the door. 'I expect Mrs Wilson has put you in your usual room. William will probably have already taken your luggage up.'

They disappeared from sight. Lucinda waited until they were no longer within hearing and then went in search of Mrs Wilson to inform her that Lord Ellesporte and a friend would be home for dinner and that they had added guests for dinner the following day. She was glad to have something sensible to do. She didn't want to think about her husband.

On her return, Eliza was reading the newspaper. She looked up.

'I was just musing how tolerant you are. Laurence comes and goes at a whim, and without warning. He should consult his wife sometimes.'

'Castleward is his home, Eliza. He doesn't need to give me any warning about what he's about to do.'

'It was good of him to invite the Stevensons.'

Lucinda extracted her embroidery from the drawer of a nearby table and made herself comfortable.

'I presume he wants to see what sort of people they are. If they are suitable acquaintances.'

Eliza's brow wrinkled.

'Do you? I thought he was merely being polite.'

Lucinda selected a thread and set to work. She was suddenly glad Eliza was present. She couldn't imagine being alone with her husband. After a short time, she put the embroidery aside and said she was going down to the lake for some fresh air.

'Do that, child, but wear a thick spencer, the wind is cool today.'

Getting to Know You

From an upper window, Laurence saw Lucinda as she strolled through the landscaped garden and beyond that, towards the lake.

She followed the edge of the water for a while and then bent to pick up pebbles and throw them to skip across the rippling waves. It was something he did, too. There was only one spot where there was a plentiful supply of pebbles, so she was already well acquainted with the vicinity.

Her looks were greatly improved, too. New clothes and a decent hairstyle helped to underline her natural elegance. Admittedly, he also liked her unassuming manner.

He almost regretted now that he had practically ignored her since they met, especially on their wedding day. His father's plans were not to his taste, and he'd tried to ignore her. That was stupid of him. They were tied for life. She already liked Guy — he could tell from her relaxed expression when she viewed him.

Timothy had just told him that the servants were in favour of their new mistress. She knew what to expect of a well-trained staff without exploiting her position. He turned away, loosened his cravat, and called for Timothy who appeared immediately with several starched replacements over his arm.

★ ★ ★

Lucinda went to her room when she returned. If Laurence wanted to talk to her, he'd no doubt send for her. Eliza was probably dozing on the chaise longue in the drawing-room, as she did every afternoon.

She picked up one of the novels she had bought in Winchester and made herself comfortable in the window niche. The sight of Laurence crossing the terrace and heading towards the stables caught her eye, and distracted her thoughts for a moment.

They all met for dinner. Lucinda changed into a close-fitting, neat dove-grey dress with lace at the neck and the edging of the puff sleeves. Molly had fixed her hair into a complicated knot and side curls. She felt confident when she joined the others.

Eliza looked at her approvingly when she came in, and she noticed Laurence nodded, too. Lucinda presumed it was the closest he would come to showing his approval. From someone who paid so much attention to his own appearance, that was praise indeed.

He wasn't a dandy, but he wanted quality, fit, style, and matching colours. Guy tended to more elaborate embroidery and embellishments, but it was never over-exaggerated so he also presented an attractive figure.

Mrs Wilson served several courses, including soup, capon, lamb, chicken pie, roasted vegetables, various cheeses, and several desserts that met everyone's approval. The dining-room was ablaze with candles, and William made sure that the service was perfect. His master didn't visit as often as he wished, but when he did, he made sure that the servants made an extra effort.

The conversation was general. Sometimes the others talked about people Lucinda had never heard of, or relatives of the Ellesporte family. Lucinda didn't mind. It was quite pleasant to sit and listen, and she learned a little more about her husband and his family history.

They moved to the drawing-room and the men drank a glass of port while they waited for coffee. Lucinda recalled some personal letters that had arrived in Laurence's absence.

'Some congratulatory letters have arrived from people I don't know,' she revealed. 'I left them on the desk. I was thinking of sending them on to you in London, but now you're here, perhaps you would like to attend to them?'

He studied her for a moment and gave her a slow smile that utterly confused her for a moment.

'Yes, I glanced through them. They are not from any close acquaintances. Perhaps you'll be good enough to reply? Just a thank you, how kind of them to write, etcetera. They will be quite happy with that.'

'If you wish, I will, of course.'

'Lucinda plays the piano beautifully,' Eliza said. 'Play for us, Lucinda.'

Lucinda felt flustered for a moment, but she rose and went to the piano.

'Would you like to choose, Eliza?'

'What about that nocturne you played the other evening? It was quite lovely.'

Lucinda thought so, too, and she was soon lost in the music. Laurence speculated as he listened, and watched her expression. He'd listened to better pianists, both amateur and professional, but she did play very well and what counted most was the fact that she felt the emotion of the piece of music she was playing.

When she finished, Guy clapped profusely and Aunt Eliza tapped the arm of the chair with her closed fan.

'That was very good,' Laurence said.

Lucinda blushed and was glad when the door opened to admit Williams and the coffee. They decided to end the evening playing cards. Lucinda and Guy lost twice and won once. Eliza won every hand. Lucinda found Laurence was a good tactician but an unenthusiastic player.

* * *

Next morning Lucinda woke early. She was not the only one. She heard movement on the other side of the dressing-room wall. She now knew that Laurence's rooms adjoined hers but she'd never entered them.

Looking out of the window, the sun was gaining strength over the morning mist covering the areas beyond the gardens. Lucinda decided it was a perfect morning for a ride.

She'd been out on her own at this time of day before, much to the disapproval of the head groom. Not because she was a bad rider, but because he thought she should be accompanied. This morning, she'd almost finished saddling her horse before the stable-hands began to appear.

Ignoring the head groom's disapproving look, and his suggestion that one of the grooms should accompany her, she set off at a moderate pace until she was beyond the boundaries of the house. The freedom of feeling the wind in her face lightened her heart.

Luckily, her old riding habit was dark blue, and the sturdy fabric had stood the test of time. She was not likely to meet anyone who knew her at this time of day, but if she did, the dark colour would satisfy anyone's standards. Her hat was undecorated; a flatter version of a man's top hat.

She was obliged to hold her whip in her right hand because there was no stirrup on that side and she needed it to help tap and guide the horse. She held the reins in her left hand. She relished always having a horse at her disposal.

At Greystone the horses had been gradually sold off when the financial situation worsened, and she had privately shed tears when someone bought her favourite mare.

Unknown to her, Laurence had ridden out before she set off. He now viewed from the top of a hill as he rested his horse under a group of trees.

When she came in view, he watched as she cantered across the open fields, avoiding any very high fences or hedges. He noticed she was heading towards him and was so intent in guiding her horse, she didn't notice his presence until she was mounting the hill towards him. Her horse snorted as she pulled at the bridle. Lucinda leaned forward to pat its head and reassure it. It gave Lucinda time to absorb his presence.

'Good morning, Laurence.'

'Good morning. You're an early bird.'

'So are you. It's a perfect time of day,

isn't it? I don't think I've ever met anyone else out at this time of day since I came to Castleward.'

She looked around while controlling her nervous mare.

'This is a lovely spot. You can see the whole countryside from here.'

He nodded.

'I didn't know you could ride, or that you enjoyed doing so.'

'We don't know much about each other, do we?' she replied, not sounding censorious.

'I used to love riding, but my father sold all the horses when the money dwindled. I had a favourite mare and I loved her very much but she had to go. Her name was Katrina.'

She stopped and wondered why she was chattering. He wouldn't be interested.

'How long ago was that?'

'Not long before Papa died. Roughly a year ago. Someone from the other side of Winchester bought her. I think he was a doctor. He seemed a nice man and I hope he gave her a good home.'

He looked into the distance.

'I can understand about getting attached. I remember feeling shattered when my father sold my favourite horse. It was a black stallion. When someone offered him an exorbitant price, he took it. I begged him not to, but he didn't take any notice, the temptation of making money was too great.'

'How old were you at the time?'

'Fourteen . . . perhaps fifteen. He didn't need the money. Sometimes I think he did it out if spite and to show me who was in control. He was an uncaring man.'

She viewed him with sympathy and nodded.

'I expect it hurt. At least my father tried to explain that he had no other choice. Perhaps your father didn't realise just how attached you were.'

He grunted.

'He knew.' His expression darkened and Lucinda tried to redirect the conversation.

'Men are still luckier in so many other ways though, aren't they? For example, I've always longed to ride astride, but my father forbade it. I read a report about a woman who did so in London. When people saw her, they declared it was quite shocking, but I envy her.' She slapped the material of her draped skirt with her riding crop. 'All this, and sitting sideways, is quite inhibiting!'

He laughed.

'I suppose it is. I've never thought about it. Now you mention it, I remember the report about that woman. She was a member of the high society and she was well known for pranks of various kinds. She took part in horse races too, until her father put a stop to it.'

'At least she knew what it felt like to ride properly,' Lucinda commented wistfully.

'Shall we return together?' he said. 'I've already been for a gallop and was about to head back to Castleward when I saw you.'

Lucinda nodded.

'I've enjoyed my run. I always try to be back before they get busy in the stables. The head groom doesn't approve of me riding on my own.'

Laurence hid his amusement and they set off side by side. Lucinda didn't know if he deliberately lessened his pace to match hers but it was pleasant to be alongside each other, and conversing naturally.

He broke their silence.

'I was just thinking about what you said about having to ride side-saddle. Why don't you get a riding habit made with the skirt split down the middle? A sort of voluminous trousers.

'Then you could ride astride and if you did meet anyone, you could slip your leg over the saddle, jump down, and all they would see is a skirt with drapes or folds. There must be clever tailors who could do that.'

Her eyes sparkled.

'Do you think that's possible? It would be wonderful.'

'Next time I go to my tailor, I'll ask

him. I imagine, the top part of the habit remains the same. Only the skirt needs to be disguised so that it looks like a skirt but is in fact trousers. Does your friend Miss Stevenson like riding, too?'

'Judith? Yes, but not as much as me. She'd be shocked to hear me wanting to ride astride. She likes docile mounts, whereas I like to race sometimes, although I try not to overrate my abilities. I avoid high-risk fences and the like.'

'She seems to be a pleasant girl.'

'She is. She's a true friend. She's an only child, like me, but she was luckier because she has never lacked for anything that was within her parents' power.

'Gradually I accepted I couldn't always have everything like she did. I didn't really mind, and Judith was never boastful or conceited. My father loved me and did his best.'

They came in sight of the house and he reined in for a moment, she followed and the horses danced on the spot as they regarded it.

'What do you think of Castleward?'

'At first, I thought I would find it difficult to fit in, but it's such a lovely house, and the estate is so well run, that I grow to like it more and more every day. Greystone will always have a special place in my heart, because I grew up there, but Castleward is a delightful substitute.

'Your agent is a very knowledgeable man, and he's always very busy but he still finds time to explain why he plants wheat in one field and barley in another, or why the field needs a new drainage ditch.

'He's also well informed about the latest agricultural developments.' She looked across at him and broke off abruptly. 'I hope you don't mind me asking him questions?'

He regarded her with a surprised expression, one that Lucinda wrongly interpreted to be condescension.

'No, by all means. I've never met a woman who was interested in the running of an estate before but, presumably, it's because you were involved in running Greystone when your father could no longer manage it himself.

'I bet Higgins is flattered, but if he thinks you are bothering him he'll say so.' Laurence was beginning to wonder what else he didn't know about his new wife. She was not at all as he expected.

Back in the house again, they hurried upstairs to change for breakfast. He knocked her door briefly later and waited. They went downstairs together.

Hostile Reaction

Guy was already eating ham and eggs, drinking coffee, and reading an out-of-date newspaper. He looked up when they came in.

'Ah, I was just wondering if I was early, or you were late.'

Laurence took his seat at the head of the table and began to butter a thick slice of bread.

'I went for a ride and met Lucinda. She'd also slipped away.'

'I say, old chap, why didn't you wake me?'

'Guy, you know you hug your bed in the mornings. My wife was company enough.'

Guy laughed softly.

'You're right, of course.' He speculated on whether Laurence was beginning to appreciate Lucinda at last.

'What are the plans for today? Are there any?'

'I have to check estate matters. You can do as you like.'

Guy turned to her.

'What are you doing, Lucinda? Will you be counting the bed-linen, dead-heading the roses, or feeding the chickens?'

Lucinda laughed.

'No, I'm going to Greystone to see how they are. I've only been there once since I married. It's only four or five miles across country.'

Laurence threw back his head and laughed.

'You don't honestly expect Guy to walk, do you? I bet he hasn't walked more than half a mile for years.'

'There is seldom a need to walk anywhere in London,' Guy retorted heatedly.

'Take the trap,' Laurence said, 'otherwise he'll be exhausted this evening.'

Lucinda nodded and winked at Guy. Laurence partook of his meal and asked Guy for part of the newspaper. When Aunt Eliza joined them, the conversation circled London news and the coming evening. Laurence left first.

Guy put his napkin aside when he noticed Lucinda getting up.

'Be honest — will I be in the way, if I come with you to Greystone? I'd like to see where you grew up.'

'Of course not. If we go by trap you'll be fresh for our dinner party.'

The journey was pleasant. Lucinda liked Guy and was happy in his company. He drove, and Lucinda didn't object, although she was quite used to driving the trap herself. He told her about his estate and about his family. He seemed especially fond of his younger sister.

When they reached Greystone, their welcome was effusive. Uncle Henry was working in the study, although he did come out to greet them. After accepting the invitation to dinner, he left them again.

Annie organised tea in the salon and Lucinda looked around nostalgically. She knew from her previous visit that Uncle Henry left the servants to their own devices.

Today she heard that the Castleward's agent had already visited various tenants and seemed to be handling the situation well, because people were co-operating. Some had agreed to try out some of his suggested ideas.

After tea Guy, guided by John, went off to inspect rebuilding work on the stables. Annie and Lucinda went upstairs to Lucinda's bedroom. Higgins had given her her pin-money, and suggested that she locked it away. She did, in her dressing-table drawer. She hadn't mentioned that she intended using some of it for Greystone.

Her old room looked beautiful. There were new carpets and bed coverings, silk curtains, and new covering on the walls. She'd chosen the materials with Annie on her last visit. The furniture had always been good — highly polished, lovingly cared for, it had been passed down for generations. She was delighted and she hugged Annie.

'It's lovely, Annie. Thank you!'

Annie's cheeks were like red apples.

'I only wish it had been like this when you lived here.'

'Ah, well, it looks good now.'

'There's enough money left to upholster the chairs in the salon, and for some new curtains. I've some sample materials, and I've been waiting for you to come, so that you can choose.'

With a nostalgic look around the room, she nodded and followed Annie downstairs. A bundle of sample materials lay in a window niche. Lucinda picked them up and they decided to recover the chairs in blue brocade and have matching darker curtains. The sage-green silk covering the walls was still good. The final result would be very pleasing.

Lucinda sighed.

'I'm so glad. Uncle Henry won't notice the difference, but if he ever gets visitors they might.'

'He has his head stuck in a book all day. I don't think he'd eat unless we reminded him.'

'And everything else is running well?'

'Yes. We're all relieved that we still

have our jobs, thanks to you. What about you? Do you like being Lady Ellesporte?' She considered her carefully. 'You look beautiful.'

Lucinda laughed.

'I now represent my social position. I'm so glad his aunt is visiting. She helped me choose my clothes, and she's good company. We don't have many visitors. My husband and Mr Mannering turned up unexpectedly yesterday.

'Mrs Stevenson and Judith were there when the two men arrived. The whole family is invited to dinner this evening and Uncle Henry, too.'

Guy returned and Annie had to explain why there were material samples spread around them. He approved of their choices. Lucinda went to remind her uncle to be punctual, and Guy walked to the waiting trap with Annie at his side.

'Goodbye, Annie,' he said.

Annie laughed and bobbed.

'Goodbye, sir. I'm glad to see that Lucinda is well.' She paused. 'I was afraid for her at first, but I should know better. She was always strong and resilient and she hasn't forgotten us, either. Using her own money to redecorate Greystone is typical. She could use it all to buy fripperies, but she didn't.'

Guy looked puzzled.

'Her own money? I thought she didn't have any money. That was one reason for the marriage — the lack of it.'

'I mean the money she gets from Lord Ellesporte to spend as she likes.'

'Oh, you mean her pin-money. I see.' He got into the trap and took the reins from the stable boy. Lucinda joined them and got in beside him.

She laughed.

'I'm afraid Uncle Henry can't be dragged from his books to say goodbye. He said he'll see you this evening. Bye, Annie, till next time.'

Guy nodded and smiled.

'It's not important.' They set off and the conversation flowed easily between them as they travelled along the lanes with their high hedging. When they reached

Castleward, Guy went in search of Laurence, and Lucinda hurried upstairs. She wanted to be sure that Molly had her dress ready for the evening.

* * *

Before long, someone knocked on the door and, without waiting, Laurence entered. Surprised, Lucinda's burgeoning smile withered and died when she noticed the hostile expression on his face. Molly was busy looking for a pair of suitable evening slippers. His expression remained intimidating.

'That's all, Molly,' Lucinda said quickly. 'I'll call you when I need you.' Molly considered his expression and departed hastily.

When she'd left, Lucinda took a deep breath.

'Is something wrong?'

His lips were a thin line and the skin over his cheeks was tight.

'I didn't give you pin-money to spend on Greystone.'

'How . . . how do you know that I have?'

'It doesn't matter how I know.'

Her face was white.

'I didn't think you sent Guy to spy on me.'

'Don't be childish. I didn't, and don't blame Guy. He just happened to tell me what he saw and what a servant told him.'

She straightened her shoulders, met his glance and tried to keep her expression under control.

'I wasn't aware my pin-money was controlled. I thought I could use it as I chose.'

'You can — within reason,' he retorted, still stiff and threatening. 'The money is for your personal expenditures and not for renovating Greystone. Hasn't Eliza explained about pin-money? Everyone knows what it's for.'

Stiffly she faced him.

'Do they? I've heard of it of course, but as I didn't move in the kind of circles where women talked of pin-money, or what they did with it, I presumed there were no rules or regulations. Wrongly, so it seems.'

His reply sounded slightly aggressive.

'If something needs improving at Greystone, tell Higgins. Anyway, there's no necessity for immediate improvements, even if it needs them. I know that. I've been there remember? As your uncle is not likely to do much entertaining, it can be spread over a longer period.'

She bit her lip, knowing he'd think it unbecoming if she argued or showed any emotion. Only her pale colour gave her away.

'I'm sorry if I've annoyed you. I didn't realise I was only allowed to spend my money on certain things.' She emphasised the 'my' and wondered if he'd retaliate. He didn't and her glance steadied as she looked up at him.

He scrutinised her silently. She couldn't tell he was already repentant. He didn't reply, turned his back, and stalked out of the room.

Lucinda noticed that her hands were

shaking. She stared at her features in the mirror and decided he must consider her stupid because she didn't realise what was normally expected. He seemed to enjoy pointing out her mistakes. Perhaps it was good that she didn't see him too often.

★ ★ ★

The evening was a success. The dinner was excellent and Laurence and Guy put their visitors at ease. Aunt Eliza chatted to Mrs Stevenson happily about London, and Lucinda kept Uncle Henry occupied by enquiring about his latest book on the Etruscans.

Lucinda looked beautiful. She'd tried hard because she was hostess at Castleward for the first time, and she didn't want to give Laurence another reason to criticise her. After dinner, the ladies retired to the salon, and the men joined them later for coffee.

Eliza suggested that Lucinda played for them again. Guy encouraged the idea heartily. She felt confident and enjoyed playing so much that it was never a millstone.

She chose a haunting melody that she often played when her mood was dulled like this evening. She still felt slightly depressed by Laurence's rebuke but avoided his glance. She let the music guide her and was rewarded by loud acclaim.

Lucinda knew that Judith had a sweet voice. It was untrained, but the lack of musical training did little to distract from the all-round attractive picture she presented. Lucinda persuaded her to sing.

Everyone complimented her, and Guy volunteered to sing a duet with her. Judith was nervous, but he had a pleasing tenor voice, and together they sounded very attractive. They were highly praised, and applauded.

Lucinda did look at Laurence while playing for them and saw a nostalgic look on his face. She wondered if he was thinking that without his father's interference, he might have been free to choose his own wife. Someone like Judith.

The Stevensons were not rich, but they had a respectable estate and a respectable income. Judith was pretty; she wasn't silly, and didn't have strange ideas like riding astride horses.

Eliza suggested they make up fours to play whist. Laurence and Uncle Henry played with Mrs Stevenson and Judith. Mr Stevenson and Guy played with Eliza and Lucinda.

The fire crackled in the grate, the candles spread their blanket of golden light throughout the room, and the sound of enjoyment flowed through the remaining hours. It was close to midnight before Laurence called for the visitors' carriages.

Laurence said farewell to his guests.

'I hope to have the pleasure of your company again soon. May I call when you're in London?'

Mr Stevenson reached out his hand.

'A pleasure, sir. We'll be pleased to welcome you. Thank you for a very agreeable evening. If you have time, stop on your way to London for some refreshments, we are on the way. My two ladies will be delighted to see you both again.' He bowed slightly in Lucinda's direction. 'Thank you, Lucinda.'

She smiled at him.

'Thank you for coming. It was lovely to see you at Castleward.'

He nodded towards Guy.

'You, too, sir. A pleasure to have met you.'

Uncle Henry joined the general exodus towards the hall. Once they were out of sight, Lucinda murmured her goodnights and hurried upstairs.

Tears of Joy

Lucinda didn't ride next morning, although she was tempted. She didn't want to meet Laurence again. Mid-morning the two men were ready to depart. Lucinda did her duty and stood on the steps to see them off.

Guy smiled and thanked her for his visit. Laurence picked up her hand and kissed it.

'I don't know when we'll be down again, but you'll continue to manage everything quite competently, I'm sure.'

'I'll do my best,' she replied with a lump in her throat.

The two men got into the travelling coach. Lucinda and Eliza watched until it was round the bend in the drive.

'Well that was all it should be, Eliza said, bustling back inside. 'I'm tired after last night. I used to celebrate until four or five o'clock in the morning, but those days have passed. I'm going to have a rest.'

Lucinda laughed.

'Do! I'm going for a walk. It's such lovely weather. Perhaps we'll share tea when I get back?'

'I should be fit again by then. Don't go too far. You should take your maid with you, but I don't suppose you will?'

Lucinda shook her head.

'I'm walking to the vicarage. The vicar's wife mentioned that she wants to organise school lessons for the village children. I want to find out what she plans to do. Perhaps I can help.'

Eliza looked quizzical.

'I don't think Laurence would approve of you getting involved. Perhaps you ought to talk to him first.'

'I don't think Laurence cares what I do,' Lucinda retorted, eyeing her steadfastly, 'as long as it costs him nothing and I don't do anything stupid. Helping to teach village children to read and write is not a stupid pastime, even for Lady Ellesporte.'

A week later, Judith called to say goodbye before she left for London. Since the evening invitation to dinner, Judith had already called once, and they went riding.

Judith mentioned the evening meal at Castleward again.

'It was so comfortable. I didn't feel at all nervous. Your husband and Mr Mannering made everything so casual and right. If my season in London is like that, I'll be completely happy. I think Mama and Papa are hoping I'll make a suitable match,' she added quietly, 'but I'll not be disappointed if that doesn't happen.'

Lucinda hugged her friend.

'You'll be a success, of course you will. I'm sure that your papa will have to fight off all the men calling at your door.'

Judith's nose wrinkled in amusement.

'You do say such funny things, Lucinda. I'm going to miss you so much, but I promise I'll write as often as I can and describe all I've seen or done.' Judith looked pensive.

'I wish you were coming. Mama says the Ellesportes have a town house in Grosvenor Square.'

Lucinda shook her head.

'I am happy here, Judith.' She pushed the beginnings of envy from her mind. She'd agreed that she and Laurence would lead different lives in different places, and she'd stick to that. She wasn't unhappy, although it would have been nice to see London and all the entertainments, just once.

★ ★ ★

At first Judith's letters were regular highlights in Lucinda's life. They were full of description, and Laurence and Guy were mentioned regularly. She wrote of evening soirées, theatre visits, private dinners, and assemblies. Then the letters became less frequent because there were too many entertainments and little time for letter-writing.

Lucinda could tell that Judith's coming-out was a success. She wrote casually that the younger son of a marquis had sent her a posy of white roses, and another young man, a captain in the dragoons, had approached her father.

As he was penniless, and had little prospect of improving his lot within his regiment, her father had immediately dampened his hopes. Judith stated that she wasn't sorry. He was pleasant, but he didn't set her heart fluttering.

Lucinda noticed how often she mentioned Laurence. How they met, and how other girls were envious of the attention she was receiving.

Lucinda mused that perhaps Laurence was already regretting their marriage. He would never act improperly but he could take a mistress or sustain a clandestine affair. What was unacceptable in the country was tolerated in London. As Laurence sent no letters, she had no idea what he was doing or what he thought.

She was surprised one day when Laurence arrived without warning. His boots and clothes were covered in dust.

'I know I should give warning,' he said after perfunctory greetings, 'but something needs my urgent attention.'

Feeling flustered by his unexpected appearance, Lucinda considered his face. He looked worried. She straightened.

'This is your home. You can come and go as you please, without warning.'

There was an expression in his eyes that Lucinda found hard to define.

'Miss Stevenson sends her best wishes,' he announced. 'I met her in Hyde Park just before I left. She was full of beans and told me all about her visit to Vauxhall the previous evening.'

Her heart skipped a beat and she searched for a fitting reply.

'She writes often. I think she's enjoying the season.'

He nodded.

'She's a great success. Her beauty and her innocence draw the attention of all the men she meets.'

She ignored the tightness in her chest.

'I'm not surprised. Would you like some refreshments?' She moved towards the bell.

'No, I'll take a bath and join you for dinner. Where is Eliza?'

'She's showing Molly how to pleat some material to make roses.'

He slapped his thigh with his riding whip.

'Right.' He turned away. 'Oh, I nearly forgot . . . I gave Higgins instructions before I left last time. He just told me he has managed to fulfil the task. You'll be interested and find him in the stable yard.' With that, he left.

Curious, she found Higgins was talking to the head groom in the stables. Lucinda entered the dark interior, and greeted them. She heard familiar whinnying from the stalls.

Her pulse skipped several beats and she rushed past them. It really was her beloved Katrina. The breath caught in her throat. She stroked the mare and felt its excitement. The agent joined her.

'A nice little mare and anyone can tell she still remembers you, my lady.'

'Where did you find her?' she asked, still feeling a little breathless.

'Last time Lord Ellesporte was here, he told me to search for her. It wasn't easy. There are lots of doctors the other side of Winchester. We started in Winchester and then fanned out further and further, until we found the right doctor, living the other side of Basingstoke.

'He didn't want to part with her, but when our man explained, he agreed. He was given a generous price, my lady. Lord Ellesporte told me to pay whatever was needed.'

Lucinda felt the tears at the back of her eyes. No-one had ever done anything as kind for her before. She didn't even realise that Laurence had listened so closely that morning when they rode together.

After a couple of minutes of patting and stroking, she turned to the head groom.

'Give her an extra ration, please.'

He touched his forehead.

'Will do, my lady, and we'll give her a good brush down.'

She returned to the house, met Eliza in the hall and told her what Laurence had done.

'Good heavens! That was kind of him. I thank God that Laurence isn't like my brother. Darrell was a penny pincher from the cradle to the grave.'

Lucinda flew upstairs and Molly helped her get ready for dinner in a pale lavender dress with a high waist, long sleeves buttoned tightly at her wrist, some embroidery on the hem, and a hint of cream lace around the square neckline.

Molly pinned up her hair in a mass of curls on each side of a middle parting. The mirror told her she looked very presentable. Her only jewellery was a necklace of seed pearls that she'd

148

inherited from her mother.

She waited for Laurence to join them for dinner.

'Laurence, thank you!' she exclaimed, before he had barely entered the room. 'I didn't realise you remembered how much I loved my horse. Having Katrina again is wonderful. It was extremely kind.'

He took a pinch of snuff and the lace at his wrist fell back. His expression was indulgent and almost amused.

'I just told Higgins to find the horse if he could, Lucinda. The agent did the actual work, not me.'

'But you told him to. Otherwise nothing would have happened.'

'I'm glad if you're pleased. It's not worth mentioning. Perhaps you'll entertain me with some piano playing this evening. That will be thanks enough.' He looked at her and his gaze hovered on her neck. 'I must remember to bring you the family jewels for you next time I come. Are you ready, Eliza? Shall we go into dinner?'

He offered his elbows and, with Eliza

on one side and Lucinda on the other, they moved into the dining-room where William was berating a maid for placing a soup tureen in the wrong position on the table

Laurence told Eliza the latest London gossip during the meal. When he chose, he was entertaining, and the fact that they were just an intimate trio made the evening more pleasant.

They withdrew to the drawing-room, where Laurence drank a glass of cognac and Eliza and Lucinda had coffee. Afterwards, with a glance in Laurence's direction, Lucinda rose and went to the piano. She played a recent piece of music she'd bought on visit to Winchester.

Laurence's eyes were on her the whole time.

'That's by Mozart, isn't it?' he commented.

'Yes, do you know it?'

'I'm not sure, but I recognise the style. I'm no expert.'

Lucinda smiled.

'Now I'll play some Scottish and Irish jigs. I'm sure you've heard most of them before.' Her hands flew lightly over the keyboard, and Eliza's fan tapped the edge of her chair. His expression was relaxed, and he viewed her with interest as the candlelight mirrored on the fine bronze sheen of her hair.

'It's a pity we are not in an assembly room,' he commented when she paused for a moment. 'I'm sure everyone would want to dance.'

She twisted sideways on the piano stool.

'Do you enjoy dancing?'

'Not very much.' He held his pince-nez and considered her face. 'Do you . . . enjoy dancing? You like playing the piano, that is clear, but dancing and piano playing are different categories.'

She smiled gently.

'I've not attended many dances or danced much. The local assemblies are usually overcrowded, and many girls are hoping for a partner. I find most of the men want to talk about hunting, or fishing. Even if you're lucky, sometimes your partner is so unskilled that you end up afterwards with bruised feet for two weeks.'

He laughed and nodded. He wondered why he felt regret that she hadn't experienced a London season. He was sure she'd have been a success. She was not a gabster. She was full of intelligent remarks and she used information with discrimination. She was also self-confident, especially when she knew the person she was with.

Eliza nodded.

'Yes, I remember the local assemblies. I went to them until I was old enough for my presentation. Then I met my husband.'

Lucinda swivelled back to the piano and began to play again. She played from memory a piece of music she loved and her two listeners were wrapped in their own thoughts for a few moments. Finally, she closed the lid and stood up.

Laurence did too.

'Thank you. That was quite delightful.'

'It was my pleasure,' she replied, almost shyly. 'Thank you for finding Katrina.'

'There was another thing you mentioned that day . . . ' he added, with a twinkle in his eye. 'We'll do something about that another time.' He studied the clock on the mantelpiece.

'I'll leave early tomorrow, so I say my goodbyes this evening. If I've time, I'll call on the return journey. I find Castleward has lost its atmosphere of gloom and doom. It's a place I enjoy being again.' He turned on his heel and left them.

Bad Tidings

Laurence had left before Lucinda got up, and for the first time she felt a real sense of loss. He was always polite, a fraction too stiff, and always aware of his social status but last night he was more relaxed than she could ever remember.

She shook off the idea how she would have enjoyed a morning ride with him. She decided to ride to Greystone to show Katrina to Annie and the others. Lucinda still couldn't believe Laurence had been so considerate.

Several days passed. She went with Eliza to Winchester again and they stayed overnight. They enjoyed the change of scenery and Lucinda bought some books and several other items she fancied.

On their return, Lucinda busied herself with helping the vicar's wife organise classes for the village children.

Mrs Walton insisted it was not fitting for Lucinda to teach the children herself, but the daughter of the local apothecary was well-educated and prepared to give lessons twice a week for a few pennies.

It was a difficult task to persuade the parents to let their children attend. Simple jobs, like watching the geese, fetching water, collecting firewood and berries, looking after younger siblings, delivering food to the fieldworkers, were all tasks given to children. It was easier to convince the mothers than the fathers. The local farmers declared outright that it was a waste of time.

'That's because most of them cannot read or write themselves, or only have minimum skills,' Mrs Walton declared. 'They are not interested in having children in the village who are cleverer than they are, and may grow up to demand more than their parents ever did.'

Eliza viewed all the happenings with some scepticism but gave in and supported Lucinda. When they talked to the parents, Eliza's forthright character and commanding attitude often persuaded reluctant parents to agree much faster than they normally would have.

One evening, Eliza and Lucinda were playing cribbage in the drawing room when they heard sounds outside. Lucinda's heart skipped a beat. She thought it might be Laurence returning, as he'd promised.

Heavy footsteps followed muffled voices and then the door flew open and William announced Guy. Lucinda had never seen Guy in disarray, but now his driving coat with its many folds looked crumpled and his top-boots were covered in dust.

She buried her surprise and disappointment, and smiled at his worried expression.

'Guy! What a pleasant surprise. William, fetch some refreshments, please.' William left and Lucinda gestured towards a fireside chair. 'You're in a mighty hurry, Guy. Sit down, and take off your coat.'

He shook his head.

'I must leave again as soon as possible. I must inform Laurence's superiors in London. I hope I can persuade them to act immediately before it's too late. I'm sure Laurence would also want you to know what has happened, just in case.'

Clasping her hands tightly she noted the agitation in his face.

'Guy, what is this all about? I didn't know Laurence had superiors and what are you talking about?'

Guy ran his hand over his face.

'Laurence has been working for the Foreign Office for over a year. No-one trusts the French and our government has spies in France collecting information about things like troop movements, political aims, personal involvements, that sort of thing.

'These spies need to get the information back to London, so they employ someone who seems innocent enough, but who is actually a courier. Laurence is one. He'd made up his mind to stop doing so, some time ago, but they persuaded him to carry on until they had a suitable replacement.'

Lucinda felt shocked but tried to appear unconcerned.

'And what exactly has happened?'

'Some group of ex-Revolutionaries had him arrested. He's in Rouen. They suspect he's carrying a secret report about the naval strength in the area.'

Lucinda heard Eliza gasp, but tried to remain calm.

'And did he have this report on him when they arrested him?'

'Yes, but they couldn't find it. The innkeeper told me they even tore his coat apart looking for a hidden pocket, but they didn't find anything. They're waiting for instructions from Paris on what to do with him. Apparently, Laurence and I had been under observation ever since we landed in France.'

'You were with him? You were together?'

'Yes, I was this time. Officially I'm not involved. It was the first time Laurence allowed me to accompany him and I was out when he was arrested. Apparently, they noticed he was visiting France regularly without a plausible reason. Laurence bought wine a couple of times, and he pretended he was interested in buying a house in Calais once, but most of the time he had no real excuse.'

'Did you see him before you left?'

'They wouldn't let me. I decided to return post-haste to get the authorities involved.'

William returned with a tray with bread, butter, some cold meats, and a jug of ale. He bowed and withdrew and Guy ate quickly. He was clearly very hungry. He looked at the mantel clock.

'They will have saddled a fresh horse by now and I'll be off. I want to be in London early tomorrow morning.'

Lucinda stood with thoughts tumbling through her brain. Finally, she spoke.

'And I'll go France. I'll travel to Dieppe by boat, and from there to Rouen. They can't deny a wife entry when she wants to visit her husband.'

Guy eyed her with astonishment.

'You don't know what these people are like, Lucinda. It's not likely that they'll allow you to visit him. They are often very objectionable.'

Eliza stared at her with an open mouth and her eyes wide.

'And how will you manage? You haven't even been outside the place you were born. You haven't been to London. You're proposing to besiege some foreign people with your entreaties — people who hate the English.'

Lucinda tossed her head.

'I'll manage. My French is good, and people are people everywhere. Perhaps I can persuade them that Laurence is innocent. It's worth a try. I've enough money to get me there, and I'm going.

'I refuse to sit here, waiting until some uncaring diplomat in London does something.' She turned to Guy. 'Do your best on the diplomatic scene, Guy. I'll do my best in Rouen.'

Eliza stood up.

'If you're determined to go, I'm coming with you, my child. My French

160

is deplorable, but I hope yours is good enough for both of us. I'll act as a suitable chaperone. I'm certain that Laurence would not want you to go anywhere unaccompanied.'

Lucinda nodded.

'I will love to have your company, Eliza. I am determined to use any method I can to get Laurence out of prison.'

Eliza's eyes sparkled.

'I haven't felt so excited since George and I had some of our adventures.'

Lucinda noted the details, from a very reluctant Guy. He also made them promise not to take any risk and end up in a dangerous situation themselves. He promised to return to Castleward as soon as he'd contacted the Foreign Office.

He didn't say so, but he was worried in case the government didn't react fast enough. As a mere courier, Laurence was not high in the hierarchy of importance. Guy promised to follow them to Rouen if they were not in Castleward on his return.

After he left, panic hit Lucinda for a moment. She tried to imagine life without Laurence and it looked very empty. Eliza's voice calmed her, and activity filled the following hours. Lucinda went straight to instruct the stables to get the coach ready to leave at dawn.

Eliza warned Lucinda they had to have plenty of money for such an undertaking. Lucinda had the remains of her pin-money but Eliza had very little. Mr Higgins was perplexed when Lucinda requested money, until she explained that Laurence needed money, and was in France.

'I want to take it to him, but don't tell the other servants. They will believe Mrs Thursby and I are visiting Newhaven. I'll return soon with my husband.'

He could tell she was being frank and fetched a strongbox from a locked corner cupboard. He handed her several bundles of notes.

'That's about five hundred pounds,

my lady. Will it suffice?'

Lucinda shoved it haphazardly into her reticule.

'I imagine so. Give me a pen, Mr Higgins. I'll give you a receipt, so that your accounts are in order.'

Lucinda scribbled a few lines and urged him again to dampen any silly rumours amongst the servants. She turned on her heel and left. Mr Higgins was impressed. She was not the docile, indolent, heartless person that most women in a similar position usually were.

* * *

The journey began at the break of dawn next morning and they made swift progress. The travelling coach was well-sprung but the roads were sometimes deplorable and they were thoroughly jostled by the time they reached the best inn in Newhaven.

Lucinda ordered the driver to return to Castleward. They went inside with

163

their sparse luggage, and hurried down a long corridor to leave again via the rear yard.

Eliza knew Newhaven and led the way to the harbour. They finally managed to find a fisherman who was prepared to set sail at once and take them to Dieppe. Eliza bargained and squabbled with him for a fair price.

The wind was favourable. He promised they would be in Dieppe before nightfall. The wind might have been favourable, but the two women found the pitching and lurching straight after the coach ride harrowing.

Lucinda sat and tried not to watch the waves. She held her smelling salts tightly in her hand and struggled to concentrate on other things such as what they would do when they arrived.

Eliza groaned and looked deathly pale. The fisherman and his mate viewed them and grinned. Both women were decidedly relieved when they reached Dieppe.

A well-dressed lady out walking her dog recommended Le Coq Rouge, as it was respectable and clean. She told them how to get there.

Their room, under the eaves, was quiet and pleasing. Neither of them believed they could eat anything, but solid ground under their feet and hunger emerged to re-kindled their appetites.

They ate in the parlour and Lucinda was pleased to find her French was still good, and she soon began to translate the conversations taking place around them, for Eliza's benefit.

They went for a short walk before daylight faded completely. The inn was in a respectable part of the town. The fresh air removed any remaining queasiness. When they returned, the maid had already turned down the bed and they readied themselves for the night.

Soon Eliza's quiet, regular breathing filled the air. Lucinda couldn't sleep for a long time. Her thoughts dwelt on how Laurence was coping, locked away in a foreign jail, in a foreign country. Lucinda was surprised how much the idea pained her. She prayed they'd find

him in time before he was moved
somewhere else. His fate was so
uncertain.

A Dangerous Mission

The crowing of a cockerel proclaimed it was time for them to get up. A glance out of the window at the red and gold colours of the dawn told Lucinda the day ahead would be fine.

Eliza clung to her pillow and declared it was an unholy time of day, but Lucinda hurried her along and soon they were dressed and in a private parlour with hot coffee in bowl-like cup, chunks of bread with honey, and some slices of ham. Lucinda questioned the innkeeper how they could get to Rouen.

He scratched his head and then fiddled with his apron.

'Two ladies, unattended? If you can afford it, it's be best to hire a coach. Public coaches are unpunctual and overfull. The roads are not good, either.'

Eliza listened to Lucinda's translation and groaned.

167

Lucinda gave him a beseeching smile, and asked him to arrange for a coach as soon as possible. He promised to do so and sent a boy to find an honest coachman who would drive two Englishwomen to Rouen.

They packed their belongings, paid the bill, and waited for their transport to arrive for the next stage of the journey.

It proved to be just as trying. Eliza commented that the French may have had a successful revolution, but not much had been done to improve road conditions since then.

When they reached the centre of Rouen, they asked for directions to the central jail and got some strange looks in return. Once they were in the area, they walked the smelly streets, looking for respectable lodgings.

The whole district was not inviting, and they finally decided on a small inn that had some bright geraniums in a pot outside the door.

The innkeeper's wife viewed them

sceptically, but when Lucinda declared they would pay in advance for a week, and that they wanted meals, she hurried to show them her 'best' room. It was poky, but it was fairly clean.

'This whole area is so disgusting,' Eliza declared. 'I had visions of sleeping in my cloak, but this place is halfway bearable.'

Molly had sewn extra pockets in the hems of Eliza and Lucinda's dresses, to store their money safely. They could now leave their luggage in their rooms without fear that if their portmanteaux were stolen, they would end up penniless.

Lucinda decided not to ask the landlady for directions. She might decide to throw them out if they mentioned the jail. They set off, walked the maze of stinking streets, and asked others for directions.

Lucinda's heart beat fast when they finally stood in front of the solid entrance door with its thick planks, artless heavy nails, and grid-iron window. She jerked determinedly on the bell fixed to the wall and waited.

Some minutes passed, and she was about to pull the rope again, when a wooden flap behind the iron grid opened.

'What do you want?' The voice was bored, harsh, and annoyed.

'My name is Lady Lucinda Ellesporte. I want to see my husband.'

'Do you? Well, you can't. He's a prisoner. He's not allowed visitors.'

'Then I demand to see whoever is in charge. I am his wife, and this lady is his aunt. We have the right to see him. He has done nothing illegal and you're imprisoning him wrongly.'

'Hah! So . . . he's just another virtuous noble Englishman we nasty French have under control, is he? His head deserves to fall under the blade of the guillotine, otherwise he'd not be here.'

Lucinda flinched, as he continued.

'He is to be taken to Paris for further interrogation. We're just waiting for those orders. We know how to treat aristocracy in France. One day the English will rise up and wipe all you nobles off the earth too. The American colonies are throwing off the English yoke already.'

'Don't be ridiculous. English people are far too sensible, and our parliament is more far-sighted than your rulers ever were. I'll not argue with you. I want to talk to whoever is in charge here in Rouen. What's his name? Is he here in the prison building?'

His voice was bullying in tone but he was clearly bored with the situation.

'Go to the Hotel de Ville, and ask for Monsieur Valdois. I doubt if he'll be sympathetic, he was in charge of our local committee during the Revolution. He decides such things.'

Lucinda could see Eliza was bristling and about to join in. She turned away and grabbed Eliza's arm.

'Let's go to the Hotel de Ville, Eliza. We'll get no sense, or any help, from this man. It's obvious that he won't let us in.'

The face behind the grill clearly understood enough English to snigger at the remark.

They asked for directions and hurried along. On the way, Lucinda was busy with her own thoughts. She began to realise that getting access to Laurence was not just a simple case of asking for, and getting, permission. A few minutes later, she turned to her companion.

'Eliza, we must return to our rooms for a while, before we go to the Hotel de Ville.'

'What for?'

'You'll see.'

In their bedroom, she folded her soft shawl into a thick square.

'Have you got ribbon or any long pieces of lacing, Eliza?'

'What for?' Eliza asked, puzzled. She ruffled through her belongings and handed Lucinda what she had.

Lucinda knotted them together with her own strings to make a long length and lifted her dress. Placing the wad of the shawl under her slip on her stomach, she tied it firmly in place with the lacing. She patted it into a smoother shape.

Eliza looked on in astonishment when Lucinda's dress fell back into place. There was a visible rounded form near her stomach whenever she moved. Eliza was startled for a moment, but then she let out a peal of laughter.

'You're going to tell them you're pregnant, to waken their sympathy?'

Lucinda nodded.

'I'm also going to tell this man that we have three other children at home,' she said quite nonchalantly.

Eliza grabbed the post of the bed and broke out in flamboyant laughter again.

'Our landlady won't notice any difference. We arrived in travelling garb, and we sat when she brought us coffee this morning. The jailer only saw my face. Even a fervent former revolutionary would never go so far as to check a pregnant woman.'

Lucinda was more nervous than she looked. At the Hotel de Ville a scruffy man in the foyer viewed them disparagingly and pointed to the stairs.

'Room at the end of the corridor. He

won't be pleased to see you.'

They ignored him, climbed the grimy steps, and marched determinedly towards the door in question. Lucinda knocked but there was no reaction. She knocked again more forcefully, and was rewarded by the door being flung open by a middle-aged man with greasy shoulder-length hair. He stared at them with angry protruding eyes.

'What do you want? Who are you?' He turned away and Lucinda and Eliza followed him inside. He plonked himself down behind the desk and reached forward for a half-chewed chicken leg on a pewter plate in front of him. The room was full of piles of dust-covered papers. The windows needed cleaning and the red velvet curtains looked as though they were very neglected.

He didn't ask them to sit down, but Eliza grabbed a dirty chair and indicated that Lucinda should, too. Lucinda sat down with exaggerated care and smoothed her dress over her rounded stomach. She waited.

'What do you want?' He chewed on the chicken and picked at bits stuck in his teeth, with dirty fingernails,

'I'm sure you're extremely busy, Monsieur Valdois, and we apologise for interrupting you, but I beg you to help us. My husband, Lord Laurence Ellesporte, is in your jail, and I'm here to beg you to show leniency. I don't know what the charges are, but I hope you'll show mercy.'

'He's accused of spying for England.'

'Spying? That is ridiculous!' She took a handkerchief from her reticule. 'That's impossible, monsieur. My husband is pleasure-loving, timid, and unfaithful. He had to flee England because he has run up unbelievable gambling debts. Our estate is terribly encumbered, and badly managed.

'If you keep him in prison, my children and I will be helpless. He has used the income from the estate for gambling and being unfaithful to me with some dreadful women, but somehow until now I've always managed to persuade him to give me enough money to cover our

175

needs.' She dabbed her nose and mouth gently. 'I've three children at home, and another on the way.'

He gestured towards her with a chicken bone.

'Then you should be glad to be rid of him.'

'If he does not return to England, the estate will be declared bankrupt, and a distant cousin will probably take over. He's ruthless and hard-hearted. He'll turn me and my children out, without a qualm.

'I beg you to think of my poor children. My husband is worthless, but he's all I've got between poverty and disgrace. He's not intelligent enough to be a spy. He has no interest in politics. If you ask him, he probably can't even tell you the name of our present Prime Minister.'

He eyed them.

'For someone who is impoverished, you're very richly dressed.'

Lucinda looked across at Eliza. She dabbed her eyes.

'Only through the kindness of this lady. She paid for these clothes. Please, sir! Have you evidence that he's a spy?'

'The case is being considered,' he retorted evasively. 'He may be sent to Paris for questioning.'

'Who reported him?'

A loyal citizen saw him talking to someone who has dealings with a group of royalist supporters. I must emphasise I am referring to the old kind of royalists!'

'Where?'

'In a reputable inn, here in Rouen.'

'Pah! Then your accuser probably didn't realise that my husband was just an inveterate gambler looking for a rich victim. Do you have any incriminating evidence?'

He leaned back into the squeaking chair.

'Well . . . no, otherwise he'd be in Paris by now.'

'There!' she declared triumphantly. 'You see! Please, Monsieur Valdois, have pity on this despairing mother.

Please question him yourself. I'm sure your excellent judgement will show you he's harmless.'

He rubbed his chin and considered her for a moment.

'Perhaps, perhaps not. I am very busy.'

'I am sure you are, but just think how embarrassing it will be if the English government make a fuss about his unjustified imprisonment. If his internment creates yet another international crisis between London and Paris, your superiors will blame you.'

He rose.

'I'll decide what to do with him, but you must now excuse me. I have a very important meeting.'

'While we await your decision, I would like to visit and take him food and clean clothes. He's my husband, I cannot desert him.' She dabbed her eyes again.

He delayed for a moment.

'Oh, very well — but for a short time, and only you — not this other woman, whoever she is.'

'I am eternally grateful, sir! Perhaps

you will give me a permit? The jailer won't allow entry without one.'

Exasperated, he wrenched open a drawer and grabbed a piece of paper.

'What's your name?'

'Lady Lucinda Ellesporte. And thank you so much! Thank you! Thank you!' She picked up her bonnet and put it on again.

He scribbled and handed her the paper.

'Half an hour! You are only allowed to give him food and clothes, and only after the jailer has checked everything first.'

Lucinda had to stop herself grabbing the paper.

'Come, Eliza, we will leave this man to his important business.' She tripped to the door and Eliza followed in her wake.

'What did you tell him?' Eliza hissed.

Outside, Lucinda felt the sweat running down her back and her knees felt weak. She gave Eliza a quick summary.

Eliza's voice was shrill with laughter. Lucinda had to quieten her.

'You told him Laurence was a bounder, that you had three children and another on the way, that he was almost bankrupt, and that he wasn't intelligent enough to be a spy?'

'Yes, I didn't think we would have a chance to see him unless I told a load of lies. You see yourself what they are like, even though you might not understand all they say.'

'My French is not up to much, admittedly, but did you need to go that far? How do you know they haven't questioned him already?'

'Because he didn't blink an eye when I asked if he had been questioned. He admitted they had found nothing incriminating. If he'd found something to implicate Laurence already, he'd have thrown us out, pregnant or no.' She hesitated for a moment. 'I'm sorry, Eliza, but he said he'll only allow me to visit Laurence, and only for half an hour.'

Eliza looked disappointed but she brushed the words aside.

'It's important that he sees one of us and you're his wife.'

Lies and Kisses

'We must buy some clothes and food. Let's find some shops.'

It was early afternoon when they returned to the jail. Lucinda tugged the bell again and the same man opened the flap in the door.

'Oh, it's you two again. I told you visitors are not allowed.'

Lucinda waved the paper in his face.

'Monsieur Valdois gave me a permit to visit my husband for half an hour. I've some clothes and food with me and I am allowed to take it to him.'

He looked disgruntled.

'Give me the paper.' He snatched it out of her hand and muttered as he held it close to his face.

It made her wonder if he could read. There was a rattling of keys and the heavy door swung open.

'I'll wait here,' Eliza said, 'and not

move a step, until you return. Give Laurence my love, and don't allow this fellow to treat you badly or I'll deal with him.' She glared at the jailer.

Lucinda hurried inside. She carried a basket with food and wine in one hand and a bundle of clothes in the other. Once she was inside, the door slammed behind her and he motioned her towards a bench.

'Let me check those things.'

He pulled each item out of the basket, examined it carefully, and left it all spread out on the bench. While Lucinda repacked everything, he proceeded to check each item of clothing she'd brought, running his hands over the seams and the pockets. He threw them aside.

'All right, let me check your bag and your cloak.' After he was quite satisfied he gestured for her to follow him.

Lucinda folded the items of clothing over her arm and followed him down a long corridor with the basket on her other arm. They went around the corner and down some winding steps.

Daylight faded as they went down below, and although there were some candles in holders on the walls, they were not lit. There were several other cell doors along another long corridor, and she followed him to the end. He fiddled with the keys until he found the right one. The door screeched as he pushed it open.

'Half an hour. No more.' She nodded and passed. He pulled the door shut after her and locked it again.

Laurence's lean figure was outlined by the weak light from the small barred window behind him. He was standing and she couldn't see his face at first, but she heard the shock in his voice.

'Good grief, Lucinda! What are you doing here?'

She walked past him and put the basket and clothes on the narrow bed. She noted that the cell was not damp, but it was cold and smelt rancid. He was only clad in breeches and a shirt. Her eyes adjusted to the sparse lighting and noticed a beard on his face. It was a foreign sight and unsettling. She ignored her own thoughts, and concentrated hard.

'We only have half an hour, and we can talk of other things if we have time, but it is very important that you listen carefully to me now.

'I went to see the man who will decide if you're to be sent to Paris for questioning, or be set free. His name is Monsieur Valdois. I told him a pack of lies just to get permission to see you. You must stick to the same story as I told him, otherwise he'll be suspicious.'

She proceeded to tell him what she had told the man.

Laurence spluttered.

'You told him we had three children and there is another on the way?' He glanced down at her round form peeping through her cloak. 'I am a wastrel, a gambler, someone who is on the brink of bankruptcy and someone who is bleeding my own estate to death. I am stupid, uncaring, and unfaithful?'

She nodded fervently.

'Exactly! I suggested that the man who accused you in that inn didn't understand that you were just looking for another prospective victim with whom you could play cards.

'You didn't realise the man you targeted was an enemy of the state and you had no other interest in him — only cards! Guy told me they didn't find the evidence they searched for when they arrested you.' She looked around the cell. 'Do you still have it?'

She heard him take a heavy breath before he replied.

'Yes, it's in the sole of my boots. They kept the rest of my clothes and then shoved me down here.'

'Well give it to me, I'll hide it. Even this jailer will never search a pregnant woman. It may be a matter of life and death that they don't find it.' She held out her hand.

After a second, he bent and removed the inner lining of his boot. He extracted a piece of folded paper, and handed it to her.

'Good.' She lifted her skirt and shoved the paper underneath the bands tying the wad of the shawl to her stomach.

He was silent for a second and viewed her with mounting amusement as she ordered her shift and her dress again, then he began to laugh. He showed no fear or despair, but perhaps he was just trying not to upset her. She sat down on the edge of the bed and joined in the laughter.

'Your aunt is with me. She sends her love. They would only allow me to visit you.' She gestured to the basket and clothes. 'We hope the clothes fit. We could only guess the size.'

He glanced at them.

'They are bound to help to keep me warm, even if they don't fit properly. And it will be the first decent meal since I came here.' He paused. 'Thank you, Lucinda. Thank you for coming, and for what you have done. I knew that Guy would go to London as soon as he knew I was imprisoned.

'I also know that the machinery in London works at a snail's pace, and I concluded that I'd be sent to Paris before anything could be done. I don't even know how much, if anything at all, London is prepared to do for me. I'm not an important link in the chain. 'I was already thinking about ending this employment when this happened.

'I've visited France too often lately, and the French are not stupid. If they notice something odd is going on, they pay attention, and when their suspicions are justified they grab and punish. I tried to act unostentatiously but they noticed.' He stroked his chin. 'I wish I could shave, it itches like mad.'

'It's obvious why they don't allow a shaving blade, isn't it?' Her eyes adjusted to the gloom and she saw the trouble in his eyes. 'You'll be freed. I'll do all I can, and Eliza will help me — you know that. I am honestly amazed that you are involved in such work.'

'I was attracted by a sense of

adventure, at a time when there was little responsibility in my life. Don't blame yourself if it goes wrong. Don't follow me to Paris if they take me there. I want you to go home to Castleward, and forget about me. That is an order, Lucinda.

'Before I left home this time, I arranged everything with my lawyer so that you'll be able to go on living as before even if I got caught and sentenced to a long-term imprisonment. I don't think they would go so far as to employ the guillotine, that might cause a diplomatic fracas, but imprisonment is possible.'

Her breath caught in her throat.

'They can't imprison you if they have no evidence, and they haven't found anything, have they? When Valdois questions you, repeat all the things I told you, and act the part. I'll bother Valdois again tomorrow and try to force him into deciding what to do. He told me he had not considered your case yet.'

He watched her silently.

'I could tell that you're not one of the pretty, clinging females who is just content to yield to a stronger will, because it's the easiest thing to do, but I didn't realise just how strong you are, that you're a fighter. You hold on like a bulldog.'

Lucinda shrugged.

'Country life is simpler. You have to solve problems fast. There is often no-one else there to provide an answer, or suggest a possible way out.'

They heard the sound of the jailer approaching. Lucinda's heart was in her mouth. She realised with sudden clarity just how much he meant to her. He was a complicated character, but he was a good one, an honest man, sincere, and candid.

He was her husband, someone who'd felt it was his duty to arrange for her well-being if things went wrong. It made her proud, and she loved him, even if he had not married her of his own free will.

The key turned in the lock, the door swung open and the jailer gestured with his thumb.

'Time's up.'

To her utter surprise, Laurence took her in his arms and kissed her on her lips. Shocked by her reaction, she noticed how it sent rivers of fire through her being. He held her at arm's length to watch her, before he drew her close and kissed her again.

'That's enough. Are you deaf? I said that time is up.'

Lucinda, picked up her reticule and walked out without a backward glance. Upstairs, he gestured towards her small bag and tipped everything out again, before he pointed to her cloak. She undid the ties and handed it to him. He searched the pockets and any seams.

Once he was satisfied, she hastily donned her cloak and followed as he crossed the corridor to the door. Eliza was waiting exactly where Lucinda left her.

'Thank goodness. I was worried every

single minute. I don't like the look of that man!'

'Neither do I, but it was all right.'

'Tell me of Laurence. How is he?'

'He pretends to be all right, but he's pessimistic about his chance of leaving the prison unscathed.'

'I don't understand why they make such a fuss. He is not a spy, just a courier. He is just a small fish in a big pond.'

Avoiding people crowding the sides of the road and the muck in the centre, they hurried back to the inn.

'A courier is a vital link,' Lucinda commented, 'and I expect they want to make an example of someone. The real spies are carefully hidden, probably French. The couriers are easier targets, because they are generally people who don't blend into the background — they pretend to be tourists, like Laurence.'

'Hmm. At least he has something decent to eat. Let's hope the clothes fit him.'

Back at the inn, the landlady promised dinner in half an hour, and the two women went upstairs to refresh and then return to the parlour where they ate alone. There were no other guests, so they were able to talk without fear of being overheard.

'I'll be so glad to get out of this harness,' Lucinda said. 'The bunched-up shawl makes me feel very uncomfortable.'

* ★ *

Next morning after a sparse breakfast, Lucinda announced they were returning to the Hotel de Ville again. On the way, Lucinda stopped to buy an onion at a stall. She peeled off the outer skin and wrapped small pieces of it in her handkerchief, before she threw the rest away.

At the Hotel de Ville, they avoided the man in the entrance hall, hurried up the steps, and down the corridor. The door was locked and there was nowhere to sit.

When Monsieur Valdois arrived a

while later, he was cheerful enough until he spotted them at the end of the corridor. His expression changed and it was full of repugnance.

'What do you want again?'

Lucinda untied the strings of her poke bonnet, patted the flattened locks into place and rummaged in her reticule for her handkerchief to dab at her eyes. It did the trick. Soon tears flowed over her cheeks.

'Good morning, Monsieur Valdois. I've come to plead with you. Please release my husband. He told me he was innocent and he'll never play cards with anyone in France again. If I cannot return with him to England, what will become of me and my children? We'll surely end up in the poorhouse.

'This lady has been very kind to me, but she had two daughters of her own, with children. She will not be able to support my family for the rest of her life.'

She dabbed her eyes again and the tears flowed once more.

'I miss my children so much but I cannot leave without my husband. I'll send for my children and bring them to the Hotel de Ville. Although they are small, my daughter and my sons will all beg you not to deny them the company of their father. Please, Monsieur Valdois, if you're not kind and charitable to my husband and my family, I don't know what I'll do.'

'Stop that snivelling and crying. I can't stand women weeping like rain from a water spout, and don't even contemplate littering this building with your offspring. I'll order that you're not allowed inside.'

'Then I'll stand outside with them, and tell passers-by and visitors why we are here.' Lucinda rubbed her eyes with her handkerchief again, and began to cry more profusely, and even louder than before. Some of the other doors on the corridor began to open. People looked out curiously and glanced in their direction.

Eliza threw her arms round Lucinda's shoulders. She awarded Monsieur

Valdois a threatening glance, and yelled at him in English as the feathers in her bonnet shook and waved in his face.

'You brute! You unfeeling French brute. Look what you're doing to this poor woman. Have you no pity? Have you no eyes in your head? She's enceinte!'

Roused to the limits of absolute rage and indignation, but also feeling like a cornered rat, he muttered under his breath and tried to think of a fitting solution.

'All right, all right! I'll consider his case today. I make no promises, because if he's guilty he must pay the price. Now go away and leave me in peace!'

Some of the doors began to close.

'And when will I be able to hear what you have decided?'

His anger was visible, his voice harsh and abrupt.

'If . . . and I say if . . . I find there is not enough evidence to detain him, I'll release him. I'll interview him sometime in the course of the day and considered the whole case before I make my decision.'

'Then I will wait outside the jail to find out what you have decided.'

He was obviously on the edge of exploding.

'No, you will not! Where are you lodging?' Lucinda told him. 'If he's released, I'll tell him where to find you, or does he know already? Now, go away and don't bother me again.'

'No, he doesn't know where we are staying. I didn't think it was important. When I visited him, there was not enough time, and I had to comfort him. He's not a brave man and he was very fearful.

'I thank you for your kindness in finding time to settle the matter today, Monsieur Valdois. May God give you wisdom, and reward you for giving my husband a fair ruling. What is your Christian name?'

He looked puzzled.

'Why? It's Nicholas, Nicholas Valdois.'

'Then if my child is a boy, I'll name him after you! Thank you, monsieur.

Heaven bless you and grant you wisdom and charity when you make your decision about my husband.' Lucinda gave him a beseeching look, and rubbed her reddened eyes again. She then tucked her arm through Eliza's and without a backward glance, they went back down the corridor.

Monsieur Valdois wiped his forehead with a dirty handkerchief, searched for his key, and unlocked the door.

'These English are all mad,' he muttered under his breath. 'The women are worse than the men.'

Free at Last!

Some hours later, Laurence walked jauntily into the inn.

'Laurence, it worked!' Eliza shrieked. 'Heavens, with that beard you look like a pirate.'

He looked at her, grinned, and ran his hand over his face.

'I know, and it feels darned uncomfortable.' He looked at Lucinda for a second or two. 'I wanted to thank my wife before, I do anything else.' He lifted her hand and kissed it.

Lucinda's heart fluttered wildly. There was a lump in her throat.

'You are free, that's wonderful.'

He held her glance.

'I don't know what you did, or what you told him, but he seemed very anxious to get rid of me. In the course of his questioning I gathered he was afraid you would continue to hang around and badger him. He was also quite derogatory about English women who didn't know their place in life.

'He asked me to explain why I came to France and what I was doing on the evening I was arrested and I just repeated the story you told me about being a gambler, and a wastrel and unable to control my addiction. I also added that I didn't deserve to have such wonderful children and such a loyal wife.'

Eliza laughed.

'She told him this morning that if he didn't decide your case soon, she'd bring those imaginary three children and stand outside his office with them, telling passers-by why you were there.'

Laurence threw back his head and laughed.

'And when Eliza joined in and started shouting at him this morning,' Lucinda added, 'I think he wondered if he was in the middle of the Revolution again. We should leave as soon as possible, Laurence. Before they change their minds.'

'I don't think that they will. He's glad

to get rid of me.' He stood tall and impressive. 'Guy has probably left my luggage with the landlord of the inn. I'll go and see if the bags are still there. Perhaps the landlord has sold everything.' He jiggled on the front of his coat. It flapped around his lean physique. 'I would like something that fits better, if possible.'

Lucinda proceeded to extract a bundle of notes from the pocket in the hem of her skirt and handed it to him.

'Then take this and buy new clothes.'

His eyes widened in surprise.

'Who taught you to hide money there?'

'No-one. We were just being sensible.'

He nodded in silent admiration.

'Once I am presentable, I'll make arrangements for our journey, and return to tell you the details.'

Lucinda nodded silently, and with a parting smile and a slight bow, he left.

Lucinda felt overwhelming happiness that he was free and that they would soon be on their way back to England and to Castleward again.

★ ★ ★

Once they set off, the journey home was uneventful. Laurence arranged it and Lucinda found that his French was excellent, much better than her own.

They travelled to Dieppe in a much more comfortable carriage than they'd had on their journey to Rouen. During their journey Laurence explained how and when he was arrested. He didn't tell them the details and Lucinda had returned the paper she'd smuggled out of his cell to him.

Dressed handsomely again, and in the fashionable elegance of dove-coloured pantaloons and a coat of blue superfine, his beard had disappeared, and his hair was tied back in its usual arrangement. He looked what he was — a handsome Englishman travelling in France.

Once or twice Laurence fell asleep for a short period in the coach. It was not in character. Usually the day was not long enough for him to accomplish all that he intended. Lucinda presumed it was because he was free from the pressure of imprisonment.

Eliza also dozed from time to time so Lucinda could study his sleeping figure and try to memorise it. He'd soon return to London and be beyond her reach again.

It was pleasant to leave arrangements to Laurence. In Dieppe, he engaged a larger boat that looked a lot cleaner. Laurence seemed to know the captain, and Lucinda wondered if he was one of the links in the chain of couriers and spies working between France and England.

Eliza had gone to lie down as soon as they left the port. Lucinda stood at the railing and ignored the motion of the boat as best she could. Laurence came to stand at her side several times, between chatting to the captain or one of the crew. The swell of the waves and ship's motion had no effect on him, he seemed to enjoy it.

'Is Eliza having a bad time?'

Lucinda brushed a strand of hair out

of her face and tucked it back under the hood of her travelling cloak.

'Yes, but I think the journey here was worse. The boat was smaller.'

He considered her carefully.

'And you feel all right? You look pale.'

She laughed softly.

'I don't think that sailing will ever attract me very much, either. I don't feel seasick but my stomach and I are arguing about which one of us is the stronger.'

He stared into the distance.

'You'll soon be able to see the coastline, and that will help you to manage the last hour or so.' He paused. 'Lucinda, I don't think I've thanked you properly for all you have done. I know how the authorities in London work — at a snail's pace. I also know Guy will do his best, but I think if you hadn't turned up I'd have been on my way to Paris by now, and then who knows what would have happened.'

'I'm glad I could help. Eliza was a great support. I intended to come on my own at first, but then she insisted on coming. She knew that a woman on her own in France would look very suspicious.' She looked up at his beloved face. 'What would you have done with the paper if things really did go wrong?'

'I would have eaten it.'

She burst into laughter and her eyes twinkled.

He grinned and she wished she could see his happy expression more often.

'Honestly, that's what I would have done. What other choice did I have? I couldn't keep it, and I couldn't bury it in my cell — someone might have found it before it rotted away.'

'Do you know what's in it?'

He shook his head.

'We just carry messages. By the way, you must never tell anyone what happened. No-one knew, or should know, I was involved in this business.'

'Of course. I'm sure Eliza won't tell anyone either, but you had better remind her. I told Higgins I was coming to France to help you but not why. The other servants think Eliza and I went to visit a friend in Newhaven.'

'I can trust Higgins. He'll be curious, but I'll make up a story about buying wine for my cellar in London, running out of money, and needing to pay the seller immediately.'

One of the crew passed them.

'You can see the coast now, sir.' He pointed. 'We've just brewed you some tea, ma'am. It's in the captain's cabin.'

Lucinda gave him a smile.

'That sounds perfect. Thank you.' She looked at Laurence. 'Shall we go?'

He held out his arm and the lace peeping out of his sleeve at the wrist ruffled in the wind. She tucked her elbow through his and he helped steady her on the way to the cabin.

★ ★ ★

Lucinda had hoped for more hours in his company, but once on land he installed them at the best inn and announced he was leaving for London.

206

'I've arranged for a coach to take you to Castleward. It will be here at ten o'clock tomorrow morning. I hope it has your approval?'

Eliza nodded.

'Yes, of course. I am glad that we are staying here for the night. The trip with that boat was quite enough for one day.'

Lucinda remained silent.

Laurence met Lucinda's eyes.

'If I leave now, I'll be in London by nightfall. Travelling by coach to Castleward and then on to London would take much longer. I want to contact Guy as soon as possible.'

She nodded.

'Please take my portmanteau to Castleward. There's nothing in it that I need, although I dread to think of my valet's complaints and reproaches.'

Lucinda hesitated but finally found enough courage to ask the all-important question.

'Then we won't see you at Castleward for a while?'

He shrugged.

'It depends on the situation. Shall I greet Miss Stevenson from you if we meet?'

She took a deep breath.

'Yes, please do, and greet Guy, too.'

Perhaps his stay in prison had heightened his awareness and he felt deeply for Judith. He couldn't offer Judith marriage, and he'd not dishonour her, but it didn't prevent him falling in love with her, even if he could only love her from afar.

Lucinda understood, and she couldn't suddenly dislike her friend just because her friend had become the object of her husband's desire.

She spent a restless night. Eliza wondered why her travelling companion was so quiet on the journey. She ought to be in high spirits after their adventure — their successful adventure.

Centre of Her Life

Lucinda found long silent walks around Castleward and things needing her attention in the house and on the estate soothed away some of her disappointment, although she thought of Laurence constantly.

On her return from France, there were two letters waiting for her from Judith, one written before Lucinda left for France, and the other a week later. They were full of details about where she'd been and who she'd seen.

The earlier one mentioned Laurence once or twice, and remarked how charming and attentive he was. She wrote that Lucinda was very lucky to have such a husband. She also mentioned Guy, and that she also enjoyed his company very much.

The second letter mentioned that she'd heard that Laurence was out of town, and was expected back in a week or two. She wished Lucinda could share the excitement of her London season, as it was so enjoyable. She'd already seen and done so much. Lucinda smiled when she read the tightly written lines.

One source of joy for her, in days that often seemed meaningless, was her daily rides with Katrina. She rode over to Greystone one morning to show her to Annie and John. They came out to admire the horse, and Katrina seemed to remember them because she whinnied loudly. Annie rushed inside to get her an apple.

'You've been lucky in your husband,' John remarked while they were waiting. 'I don't know of many men who would go to so much trouble.'

Lucinda patted her horse.

'Yes, you're right. It was very kind of him. I only mentioned it in passing and he didn't tell me what he was going to do.'

After Katrina had been handed over

to the stable boy, she went inside to greet her uncle and share a cup of tea with Annie.

The new decorations in the drawing-room looked elegant but she could only think how angry Laurence had been when he discovered she'd paid for them with her pin-money.

Annie told her about happenings in Greystone and Lucinda listened with half an ear. She mused on how she'd changed since her marriage to Laurence. Before, Greystone was the centre of her life — now it was Laurence. She must stop being depressed and worried in case he was enamoured of Judith, or some other woman. She must be grateful for what she had, a lovely home and a secure future. She dragged her attention back to Annie's chatter.

'It's time that you came out of mourning attire, my love. Your clothes are nicer than anything you could afford at one time, but you can choose more cheerful colours now.'

Lucinda nodded.

'Yes, Eliza said the same the other day. She's still reluctant to journey anywhere at the moment, but as soon as she feels recovered we will be off to Winchester again.'

Annie looked curious.

'Yes, we heard you'd gone away on a visit with his aunt.'

Servants knew everything. She'd known about the happenings at Judith's home, long before Judith told her about it herself.

'Yes, we visited friends of Eliza's,' she replied, unable to tell the whole truth, even to Annie. 'They live on the coast, and the sea air was bracing. We didn't undertake much, just walks and supper invitations, but it was an enjoyable visit. Eliza doesn't enjoy travelling very much, and she needs time to adjust before we can set off again.'

Annie nodded.

'As long as you're happy, I am happy.'

Lucinda touched her hand and there were tears at the back of her eyes. She had no reason to be unhappy, but real happiness would always be denied to her, because she could never tell Laurence that she loved him, and he would never feel the same.

★ ★ ★

Lucinda was genuinely delighted to find Guy at Castleward when she returned. Eliza was entertaining him with their story of what happened in France. He rose when she entered and took her hands in his.

'Laurence told me how you managed to get him out of that jail, but he didn't tell me all the details. Mrs Thursby has been enlightening me. You're a courageous woman, Lucinda.'

Lucinda coloured.

'My name is Eliza, young man,' Eliza retorted. 'Mrs Thursby, or Laurence's aunt, is too staid and old-fashioned.'

Guy laughed.

'As you wish, Eliza!'

'Are you staying, or are you just passing through?' Lucinda asked. 'How is Laurence?' she added, trying to sound casual. 'Has he sorted out his position with the Ministry?'

'I'll stay this evening, if I may, and be on my way tomorrow. I am travelling to my estates and to visit my family.

'Laurence is now free of responsibilities. He already wanted to quit before this happened. He felt he was being watched very carefully. The government wouldn't let him carry on any more now. His name and face are too well known. Any more trips he makes to France will be for pleasure and nothing else.'

'Well, I'm not interested in going to France. Never again!' Eliza snorted.

Lucinda laughed.

'I must change my riding outfit. When I return, perhaps you would enjoy a walk around the gardens, if you've been travelling all day?'

He smiled.

'That sounds just the thing.'

★　★　★

They strolled in the direction of the lake. She felt relaxed in his company and she could tell Guy liked her. Their conversation was general. Then she asked him about the London season and if he had seen Judith. He paused suddenly and turned to face her. Lucinda was surprised but she stopped and met his gaze.

'Yes, I saw her just before I left. In fact, I have seen her quite regularly since she came to London. She's the centre of attention wherever she goes. I don't think she'll capture a duke, but rumour has it that she'll end the season with a title to her name.'

He sounded nostalgic and looked sad. Lucinda wondered if he had fallen under Judith's spell too. Dare she ask?

'Then she's a great success?'

'She is, and that's why I left London.' He looked away.

'Because you like her too much yourself?'

'Yes, but I've little to offer in comparison to other suitors who gather at her door.'

'Oh, come, Guy! You're not a pauper. You have an estate and sufficient income. If you like her, why not talk to her father, and still more important, find out what Judith thinks. Have you mentioned anything to her?'

He shook his head.

'She's never alone, and I don't know if she thinks of me in any way other than that of a friend.'

'She always talks about you in glowing terms to me in her letters.'

'Does she?' He eyes lit up. 'But there are others, with greater incomes, titles, and connections.'

'So that means you give up before you know where you stand? I think you forget that her parents love Judith very much. They'd never force her into a marriage she didn't want.

'Judith will be able to make her own choice, and I think she already thinks more highly of you than you realise. I know Judith very well, and you need not worry that she needs a round of festivities all the time. She's enjoying her visit to town because it's her coming out, but she'd not want a lavish lifestyle.

'She wants someone who loves her, someone she can love, someone who will take care of her. You can afford the kind of comfort and entertainments Judith would enjoy.'

His cheeks were flushed.

'It would be an honour to take care of her.'

'Then decide what will be best for Judith, and for yourself. Don't be of faint heart.'

'Perhaps that is my problem. I am afraid of failure.'

'Take heart! Find out what her father thinks, and if he has no objection, I am sure he'll allow you to talk with Judith in private.' She turned towards the lake again.

'Come! It is almost time for dinner and Eliza is looking to playing cards afterwards. It's her favourite pastime.'

He laughed.

'Thank you, Lucinda — for your

encouragement.'

They spent a quiet, enjoyable evening. Eliza won all the hands, so she was more than satisfied. Lucinda could see Guy was still busy with his own thoughts but Eliza didn't seem to notice.

Lucinda and Guy shared an early breakfast. Guy told her that, just before he left, Laurence had won a wager against a fellow club member to drive to Reading and back and had had his official resignation from further government service accepted.

'But I expect Laurence has already written to you of that.'

He hadn't. Lucinda busied herself with her breakfast without answering.

She accompanied him to the main door, where his horse was saddled and waiting. He hoisted his travelling bag behind the saddle, took the reins from the waiting groom and sprang into place.

After saying his goodbyes again, he rode off at a steady pace down the long driveway. At the bend he paused and looked back. She was still watching so he waved, and she waved back. Lucinda asked the groom to saddle Katrina, and went inside to change.

A few minutes later she galloped across the countryside. It was still blanketed in the morning mist. When she reached the crest of the hill where she'd met Laurence that morning, she paused to think that her morning rides were the times when she felt most free. At Castleward, she was responsible for its well-running and she was always under observation.

* * *

Later that morning, after Eliza had finished breakfast, she declared that she was ready to go to Winchester again.

'It's time you wear lighter colours, my dear. The next time Laurence comes, you will look even more attractive.'

'I don't suppose Laurence will pay much attention, Eliza. He sees well-dressed, pretty women all the time, but

219

I think he does enjoy getting away from all the hustle and bustle of London to Castleward. He loves it more than he cares to admit.'

Eliza picked up a cup of tea.

'You may be right, but Laurence does notice what you're wearing. He's lived too long among society not to. It's a shame that you don't choose to be with him in London. I'm sure you would like it, and London would like you.'

Lucinda laughed softly. Eliza liked Laurence very much and Lucinda didn't want to spoil that relationship.

'I enjoy Winchester just as much as I would London. I'll love some new dresses and I've read all the books we bought last time we were there.'

Eliza's eyes twinkled.

'You and your books! But if it makes you happy then it's fine with me.'

★ ★ ★

Two days later, she and Eliza strolled down the main street in Winchester.

The weather was perfect. Lucinda could tell that as they walked along that Molly was hoping to meet old acquaintances, now that she was a lady's maid.

At the dressmaker's she sat quietly on the side and didn't enquire about her former colleagues in the back room. Lucinda noticed the dividing curtain twitch once or twice and knew if she wanted to, that Molly would find a way to contact them.

They ordered two new dresses, one in apple green with a high waist, beautiful embroidery on the hem and around the neckline, and another in shiny bronze silk with a bodice draped in the Grecian style. Both styles suited her beautifully.

After ordering the various materials and accessories, they returned to the inn where they shared tea. Eliza declared she'd not leave the inn again that day, but Lucinda wanted to buy some books so she set out with Molly at her side.

Lucinda choose a travel guide on Italy and two novels that the shopkeeper recommended. It was still early, and Lucinda wanted to look inside the magnificent cathedral. It wasn't far away, and when they reached the portal, she turned to Molly.

'You're free now, Molly. I'll return to the inn after I've looked around the cathedral. I think you once told me once that your mother lived near here, didn't you?'

Molly looked slightly shocked.

'It would be wrong to leave you, my lady. Mrs Thursby will upbraid me.'

'I promise you it will be all right. Go and see your mother.' She fished in her reticule and handed her a sovereign. 'This is part of your wages. I expect you'd like to help your mother.'

Molly looked at her uncertainly.

'Thank you, my lady. It's very kind of you. I was going to try to see her later after you were ready for bed.'

'Good gracious, Molly. That is too late for you to be out on the streets on your own. Go now and be careful. I'll manage very well on my own. I'm used to looking after myself. I'll see you tomorrow morning.'

Molly bobbed, stuck the gold coin in her pocket, and set off, leaving Lucinda to the bliss of being on her own and doing something she enjoyed.

* * *

Next morning, Molly smiled broadly when Lucinda asked if she had found her mother well.

'Yes, my lady. She was so pleased to see me, and so grateful for the money. Thank you again.'

Lucinda brushed the thanks aside.

'Help me with my hair, Molly. You have a knack to get it just right.'

After they'd finished breakfast, Lucinda declared she wanted to view some of the town's older buildings. She waved a pamphlet.

'I've read about some of them. We can't go inside all of them, unfortunately, but we can see all of them from the outside.'

Eliza pretended to protest.

'What on earth do you want to visit a lot of old buildings for?'

'I don't intend to waste time. I want to learn more about the town's history.'

'Do you want me to come as well, my lady?' Molly asked.

'No, Molly. Go to the dressmakers and make sure that the materials have been delivered. Ask when the dresses will be ready.'

Eliza gave in and they set off at a comfortable pace. Lucinda could tell Eliza was not the least interested, but she didn't protest much. Eliza enjoyed commenting on the dresses of other women they passed, and looking for a tea-room to sit and watch the rest of the world go by.

It was midday when they returned to the inn. Molly hurried downstairs as soon as she heard them coming.

'Lord Ellesporte is here, my lady,' she informed them breathlessly. He's in the private parlour.'

'Good heavens!' Eliza exclaimed. 'How did he know we were here?'

Lucinda followed in her tread. She felt shock, her heartbeat quickened, and colour flooded her cheeks. She was glad she was hidden behind Eliza's back. It gave her a moment to adjust before she had to face her husband.

Messages of Love

Laurence was sitting in a window niche with a tankard in his hand. Beautifully dressed in shades of grey and dark blue, he took Lucinda's breath away.

He stood up when they came in, bowed nominally to Eliza and then came across to Lucinda. He took her gloved hand and brushed the surface with his lips. Their eyes met.

'They told me at Castleward you were in Winchester,' he said, 'so I rode over this morning.'

'You rode from Castleward?' Eliza exclaimed. 'What time did you set out, Laurence?'

'Quite early this morning,' he replied. 'Riding cross-country shortens the distance a great deal.

'I wasn't sure where to find you, but I was told this was the best inn in the town, so I came straight here.

'Your maid told me you were out exploring the town.' He turned to Lucinda. 'Was it interesting?'

Still flustered by his unexpected appearance, her throat felt constricted, but she managed a reply.

'Yes, it was very interesting.' She looked at the table. 'Have you eaten?'

'No, I decided to wait for you.'

'Do you have a special reason to come?' Eliza broke in. 'Not another problem concerning France, I hope?'

He laughed softly.

'No, that's all finished.'

'Well, considering the kind of flying visits you've made since I arrived, riding to Winchester on the spur of the moment and without reason is not so unexpected.'

Laurence took his pocket watch out of his waistband and glanced at it.

'True, but perhaps you'll see me more often in future.' He pushed the watch back into place.

'I already told the innkeeper that we'll share a meal. Perhaps you will join me in a couple of minutes?'

Lucinda nodded and was glad of a chance to escape for a while. Eliza was still chatting to him as she left and hurried upstairs. Molly was waiting.

'Your slippers and silk spencer are ready, my lady. You'll not need your half-boots now, will you?'

Sitting in front of her travelling case, Lucinda looked at her face in the mirror. She patted her hair.

'No, the slippers are better. Perhaps you'll straighten these braids after I've washed my hands and face. Then I'll be fit to join the others for luncheon.'

Molly did as she asked, and by the time Lucinda descended the stairs again she had adjusted to the knowledge he was there. She just hoped that she could keep her feelings hidden.

Eliza was still in her room, and Lucinda told herself not to be cowardly. She could face her husband on her own.

She returned to the private parlour where a white tablecloth now covered the table. Various dishes were arranged on it and it was laid for three people. His face cleared as she came into the room.

'Good! I see you don't take hours to be ready.' He gestured towards the meal. 'Please! If I remember rightly, Eliza takes ages.'

'I visited her once in Brighton and persuaded her to come to one of the assemblies. I think I waited two hours until she was ready.'

Lucinda smiled.

'Yes, I know. I'm used to her. I announce things long before the actual time. In that way, I cheat her into being punctual.'

He laughed warmly.

'That is a clever strategy.'

They sat down opposite each other, and began helping themselves to some of the dishes.

Lucinda ate more sparingly than he did. He poured her a glass of wine and lifted his own. She lifted hers in return and drank a sip. It was pleasant. He noticed her expression.

'Yes, it's not too bad, is it? I expected it might be like vinegar, but the inn-keeper seems to keep a good cellar. We must come here again.'

Lucinda noted the 'we' but didn't comment.

'I thought we could ride back together to Castleward,' he announced, putting butter on a chunk of bread. 'We could be home long before dark if we set out after this meal.'

'What about Eliza?' Lucinda asked. 'I've no riding garb here, and no horse, either.'

'That's been sorted out. Eliza says she is happy to travel back tomorrow or the day after.'

Looking pleased with himself, he nodded in the direction of one of the corners.

'There's a package over there for you. Remember you said you would like to ride astride like a man? I had my tailor make you a skirt which is divided in the middle.

'I've also arranged for a good horse for you from the stables here.' He paused. 'If you prefer to travel with Eliza, then I've no objection, of course.'

Still overwhelmed, Lucinda glanced at the brown paper package, but finally she gave in to temptation.

'I don't know if I'll manage.'

His eyes twinkled.

'You'll manage. If not, we'll walk. Perhaps it would be wise for you to wear your thickest under-garments — that will probably help.'

She blushed and nodded. She felt exultant.

'How did you know my size?'

He drank a sip of wine.

'I asked your maid last time I was home. You told me that she worked in a dressmaker's previously and she gave me some very exact measurements. Why don't you try it on?' He paused. 'That's if you have finished eating, of course.'

She was too excited to eat more. Lucinda got up and grabbed the package.

The skirt was of dark green velvet and it fitted like a glove. She twirled around and knew it looked good, although she couldn't see much in the small mirror.

Molly looked shocked at the split in the skirt, but the happy expression on her mistress's face banished any words of disapproval.

Lucinda hurried back downstairs and felt a little shy as she re-entered the room. Laurence viewed her and nodded approvingly.

Eliza was there and gave an enthusiastic nod of approval.

'By Jove, that is stylish. The material is beautiful, and it's an excellent cut. It underlines that you have a nipped-in waist. Laurence tells me you're going to ride back to Castleward with him? I hope it won't be too tiring.

'One of the dresses will be ready tomorrow afternoon, so I'll wait for it, and bring it with me on Thursday, if that is all right with you?'

Lucinda couldn't tell if Eliza realised noticed the skirt was split in the middle, but she didn't care. Molly said it was so cleverly cut no-one could ever tell.

'Yes, of course. If you don't want to wait, the dressmaker will deliver it later. If you want to leave earlier just do so.'

She was too excited to wait any longer. She turned to Laurence.

'Can we leave?'

He smiled languidly.

'Yes, I've ordered our horses to be ready. They are waiting in the yard, out the back.'

Lucinda wasn't sure if they would leave the town unnoticed, but she pecked at Eliza's cheek and followed him down the corridor. Outside he turned to face her. Her pulse quickened.

'Can you ride side saddle for a while? If you ride astride through the streets it might cause an uproar. We'll pick our way through the side-streets to the outskirts, then you can take wing!'

Her colour was bright.

'Side-saddle on an ordinary saddle is probably uncomfortable, but I'll manage.'

Once they reached open fields, Laurence spread his arm in an arc.

'You can now fulfil your wish. Do you need my help to re-position?'

Lucinda gathered the thick bundle of green velvet and shook her head. She swung her inner leg over the saddle and settled. She looked across at him and smiled.

'Thank you, Laurence.' And then she set off at a gallop. He caught up with her and they rode side by side, across fields and through woods. Lucinda was delighted. She felt so balanced and in control.

Laurence viewed her excited face, and decided he had done the right thing. An hour later he suggested they paused. Reluctantly she agreed. As long as she could re-mount and carry on, she'd agree to anything!

He helped her down, and his strong hands encircled her small waist and her breath caught in her throat as she slid down his chest, and looked into his dark eyes.

There was something hidden there in their depths.

He always had his emotions under control, but at the moment his face was full of unspoken messages. He freed her.

She arranged her skirt and he tied their horses to a nearby tree. The green light filtered down on to the mossy ground and it was silent apart from the sounds of birds. He broke the silence.

'Oh, I must tell you — I nearly forgot. Your friend Judith and Guy are betrothed.'

She gazed at him in surprise.

'Really? Guy seemed very undecided on what he should do.'

He slapped his thigh with his riding crop.

'Yes, he told me what you told him. It encouraged him. After clearing the way with her father, he plucked up enough courage to talk to Judith.

'It seems there was no hesitation in her acceptance. Guy is insanely happy. I've seldom seen him so.'

She couldn't judge from the tone of his voice if the news made him unhappy, but she decided this was as good a time as any to tell him where she stood. She cleared her throat.

'I'm happy for Guy, and for Judith. He loves her, and I think that she may love him too.

'I also must tell you, Laurence, that I am fully aware that the circumstance of our marriage presents you with a problem if you form a special or lasting attachment for someone.'

She heard him draw a deep breath, but she hurried on.

'You're still young and it is likely to happen. I promise you I'll never make a fuss, because I am sure you'll choose someone with discretion and care. I'll never stand in your way.

'The only thing I ask is that you never bring your mistress to Castleward, but if that is what you wish to do, that you'll allow me to return to Greystone to live there.'

He stared at her. The skin over his

chiselled features tightened and his brow furrowed.

'Good grief! Do you think I would do such a thing? Why ever do you think so?'

She shrugged.

'You meet lots of attractive, beautiful women, and our marriage was forced on you. It's logical that you might regret that one day.' She gathered her courage.

'I even wondered if you had become enamoured of Judith, because she mentioned you often in her letters, and you have also mentioned her nearly every time we met.' Her colour was high but she met his glance.

He burst out laughing.

'Judith? Yes, I saw her very often in London. I gave her more attention than I generally would have, but only because she was your friend.

'I noticed that Guy's interest was growing, and I thought they were well suited, so I encouraged their meeting by taking Guy along with me.'

'Oh, I see. But anyway, I wanted you

to know I'll do my best to act sensibly.'

His lips twitched.

'So, you're prepared to run back to Greystone when I bring a doxy home?'

Her lips pursed.

'I've no doubt you would never bring a doxy, you have too much taste to do that. But I am quite prepared to return to my old lifestyle, if necessary.'

'I am afraid it is too late. I've already formed a strong attachment. In fact, I am in love with her, but I don't want you to withdraw to Greystone.'

A pain touched her heart, but she nodded.

'So, you will remain in London? I am happy in Castleward but I won't stand in your way if you want to bring someone else to your home.'

There was a tone of exasperation in his voice.

'Don't you wish to know who she is?'

She turned her head away and bit her lip.

'No. I'm sure I'll hear of it in due course.'

He reached out and twirled her to face him.

She looked up into his face, into the depths of his dark eyes, and she wished she didn't care. He wakened feelings of desire in her she never thought possible.

'My dear wife. It is you! I never thought love would happen to me, but it has. You're strong, you're caring, you're beautiful and you're loyal. I've never felt for anyone like I feel for you. I want to spend the rest of my life with you.

'I want you to be at my side in Castleward and in London. I love you.'

The breath went out of her lungs. Her knees were like jelly.

'Me?' she stuttered.

He gave her one of his wonderful smiles.

'Yes, it's you, my darling! We were forced into this marriage, but today I am prepared to go down on my knees and thank my father.

'I thank God that you never had a

London season, because you would have taken the town by storm.

'Do I have a chance? Do you think you could forget the uncaring way I acted in the past, and grow to like me a little, and perhaps even love me a little one day?'

'I hope this is not because you feel indebted because I came to France,' she replied, with an unsteady voice. 'You're not obligated in any way.

'I . . . I never really disliked you, Laurence. You puzzled me at first, but I soon found that I liked you. Under the cultivated, sophisticated, man, there is someone who pretends to be disinterested but is a good person.'

He eyed her for a moment.

'I swear it has nothing to do with France. For some time now, I've been drawn to Castleward again. I've not felt like that since my mother passed away. I asked myself why and realised it was because I wanted to see you.

'Every meeting strengthened the attraction and I then realised I had fallen in love with my wife. I just hope I can make you love me one day.'

She viewed him in wonderment, and summoned all her courage.

'I love you already. I've never been in love with anyone before but I only know I long for you, and want you at the centre of my life, day and night, as long as I live.'

He looked amazed for a second or two before he laughed exuberantly, picked her up and swung her around. The green velvet brushed the greenery, and he set her down before pulling her towards him and kissing her frantically.

She found herself kissing him back and rivers of fire were kindled between them. He kissed her face and then cradled her face between his large hands before he kissed her again.

They stared at each other in amazement as they realised this was just the beginning and hardly believing it was real. He pulled her to his heart.

'I know that you love the countryside,' he whispered, 'but I would like to show you London. We could then take a delayed honeymoon journey to Italy or Greece or wherever you would like to go.'

She looked at him.

'Not to France?' she quipped.

He laughed and looked jubilant.

'I think we have had enough of France for a while. We'll probably travel through it, but with you at my side it will be all pleasure.

'I also want to show you off to my friends, to say, 'Look at this beautiful woman, she's mine'. The most wonderful thing about all of this is that we are already married!'

Lucinda looked at him and laughed. Her eyes sparkled and her cheeks were the colour of roses.

'Yes, I suppose it is. I'd love to travel, and I find I would love to see London. I'll always love the countryside, but perhaps town life will appeal to me, too.'

Laurence pushed Lucinda from him, holding her at arms' length, and looked into her eyes.

'I can't find the right words to explain how happy you make me. I don't deserve you. I read that good marriages are made in heaven and I am going to do my best to make ours one of those.

'Shall we ride on to Castleward now? We have this evening, all tomorrow and part of Thursday to enjoy just being unobserved together.

'I'm so glad I can show you how much I adore you without Eliza watching us all the time.'

Lucinda laughed and then ran her hand down the side of his face.

'Please don't tell Eliza to go home again. She has been a good friend and she loves Castleward.

'She was in love with her husband, so I am sure she will be discreet when she notices we love each other, too. I'll try to make you happy, Laurence.'

He took her hand and kissed it.

'You already have made me happier than I've ever felt before. Saying you love me is more than I ever expected.

'If only you knew how hard it was for

me to gather enough courage to talk to you today.'

'You . . . you needed courage? I don't believe it.'

'This is where our life together really begins for us.' He slipped his arm around her waist and between kisses they went back to their rested horses.

She looked around.

'I wonder where this place is. We will never find this glade again.'

'It doesn't matter if we don't, does it? We've found each other.'

Laurence kissed her and helped her into the saddle. They set off and their smiles and expressions sent secret messages of love as they glanced at each other.

They were free at last to know they loved someone who loved them in return.

When they came in sight of Castleward, they viewed it together.

'We have been manoeuvred into an arranged marriage,' Laurence remarked, 'but your father and mine did the right thing, after all. Are you ready to go home? Our home?'

Lucinda smiled warmly at him and took a deep breath.

'Yes, Laurence. Let's go home.'

We do hope that you have enjoyed reading this large print book.

Did you know that all of our titles are available for purchase?

We publish a wide range of high quality large print books including:
Romances, Mysteries, Classics
General Fiction
Non Fiction and Westerns

Special interest titles available in large print are:
The Little Oxford Dictionary
Music Book, Song Book
Hymn Book, Service Book

Also available from us courtesy of Oxford University Press:
Young Readers' Dictionary
(large print edition)
Young Readers' Thesaurus
(large print edition)

For further information or a free brochure, please contact us at:
Ulverscroft Large Print Books Ltd.,
The Green, Bradgate Road, Anstey,
Leicester, LE7 7FU, England.
Tel: (00 44) **0116 236 4325**
Fax: (00 44) **0116 234 0205**

Other titles in the
Linford Romance Library:

TWICE IN A LIFETIME

Jo Bartlett

It's been eighteen months since Anna's husband Finn died. Craving space to consider her next steps, she departs the city for the Cornish coast and the isolated Myrtle Cottage. But the best-laid plans often go awry, and when Anna's beloved dog Albie leads her away from solitude and into the path of Elliott, the owner of the nearby adventure centre, their lives become intertwined. As Anna's attraction to Elliott grows, so does her guilt at betraying Finn, until she remembers his favourite piece of advice: you only live once . . .

WILD SPIRIT

Dawn Knox

It's Rae's dream to sail away across oceans on her family's boat, the *Wild Spirit* — but in 1939 the world is once again plunged into conflict, and her travel plans must be postponed. When Hitler's forces trap the Allies on the beaches of Dunkirk, Rae sails with a fleet of volunteer ships to attempt the impossible and rescue the desperate servicemen. However, her bravery places more lives than her own in jeopardy — including that of Jamie MacKenzie, the man she's known and loved for years . . .

RETURN TO TASMANIA

Alan C. Williams

Heading back from Sydney to her idyllic childhood home in Tasmania, Sandie's priorities are to recover from a bullet wound, reconsider her future in the police, and spend time with her sister and niece. But even as the plane lands, she senses that a fellow passenger is not all he seems. When a series of suspicious events follow her arrival, the mystery man reveals himself as Adam, who has been sent to protect Sandie's family as they become embroiled in the fall-out following the double-crossing of a dangerous criminal.

THE ENGLISH AU PAIR

Chrissie Loveday

Stella Lazenby flies to Spain to work as an au pair for Isabel and Ignacio Mendoza, looking after their sons Juan and Javier. The parents are charming, the boys delightful — and then there's the handsome Stefano, who becomes more than a friend . . . But all is not as perfect as it seems. Housekeeper Maria resents Stella's presence, and Isabel worries that her husband is hiding secrets. Then Stefano is accused of stealing from Ignacio's company, and Stella doesn't know what to believe . . .